Walking a Tightrope

New Writing from Asian Britain

Edited by Rehana Ahmed

YOUNG PICADOR

To my parents, Haroon and Anne Ahmed

First published 2004 by Young Picador
This edition published 2005 by Young Picador
an imprint of Pan Macmillan Ltd
20 New Wharf Road, London N1 9RR
Basingstoke and Oxford
www.panmacmillan.com

Associated companies throughout the world

ISBN 0 330 41579 4

A CIP catalogue record for this book is available from the British Library.

Typeset by Intype Libra Ltd
Printed and bound in Great Britain by Mackays of Chatham plc, Kent

Contents

Introduction

Walking a Tightrope is a lively and eclectic anthology of new stories by writers of South Asian descent living in Britain. When I asked the ten very different authors to contribute to *Walking a Tightrope*, I encouraged each of them to write the story of their choice. My aim as editor was to put together an anthology that captured the diversity of Britain's South Asian population for a contemporary multicultural readership. Because 'Asian Britain' is not a single, definable category; it encompasses a wide range of cultural backgrounds and a myriad of stories which have yet to be told.

The result is a collection that resists any fixed idea of what it is to be Asian in Britain and challenges any stereotypes about what 'Asian writing' might be. Together, the stories will take you on a kaleidoscopic journey through a multi-faceted Britain and beyond – up into the heady peaks of the Himalayas to encounter the mythical yeti, back down into the winding alleys of a small town in India, and across the boundaries of reality to the bizarre Kingdom of

Nonsense. They are, in turn, funny, thought-provoking, imaginative, unsettling, moving and captivating.

But there is of course a thread that links these ten writers – and it is here, in part, that the importance of the anthology lies. All of them trace their personal stories back to histories of colonization and journeys from South Asia to Britain. These journeys may have begun in Pakistan, Sri Lanka or India; they may have been routed through other countries or continents; they may have been experienced by the writers themselves or through the stories and memories of a previous generation. While most of the migration from South Asia to Britain took place after the Indian subcontinent and Sri Lanka won independence from British colonial rule in the late 1940s, Britain has had an Asian population for several hundred years. But those who made these journeys across continents and walked tightropes between cultures have often had to struggle to make their voices heard above racist attitudes and government policies.

Recently, however, Britain's cultural diversity has begun to be celebrated and today South Asian writers and artists are making an impact. Monica Ali's *Brick Lane*, and the novels of Salman Rushdie and Hanif Kureishi; Meera Syal and Sanjeev Bhaskar's popular television series *Goodness Gracious Me* and *The Kumars at No 42*; the music of Nitin Sawhney, Asian Dub Foundation and Panjabi MC; Ayub Khan-Din's *East is East* and Gurinder Chadha's *Bend It Like Beckham*: these are just some examples of the outstanding talent that has emerged in recent years.

While anthologies of South Asian writing have been published, collections of stories by Asian writers *based in Britain* have been less visible and slower to appear. There has also been relatively little fiction for younger readers by Britain's Asian writers. The brilliant and varied novels and poems of Jamila Gavin, Farrukh Dhondy, Debjani Chatterjee and Bali Rai have helped to fill this gap; *Walking a Tightrope* is, I believe, another important step in this direction. For especially in today's climate of fear and misunderstanding between East and West, it is essential that more Asian voices are heard in Britain, and that more stories are told.

This collection will, I hope, offer all readers stories that will both resonate with their own experiences and open up windows on to less familiar worlds. You will meet Asha, who tries to reconcile the pressures of her strict father with her desperate desire to get in with the cool crowd at school; Dilip, whose passion for playing the drums offers him an escape from the warring gangs that rule his estate; Shah Bano, who has a huge crush on her brother's best friend, Feroze, but can't understand his decision to join the army; and Murad, who learns that to love Tsuru he must let her keep her secrets. You will find hard-hitting stories of domestic violence and the bleak realities of war; and hopeful stories in which a second and third generation of young British Asians meet the challenges of growing up in more than one culture with energy and humour – and discover both the complexity and richness of experience that this can bring.

I was delighted that such a broad spectrum of writers were keen to contribute a story to *Walking a Tightrope*. Some are established children's writers, while others have not written for younger readers before; some are best known for their short stories, while others are turning their hand to this genre for the first time. All have responded

3

to this project with tremendous creativity and energy. *Walking a Tightrope* is testimony to their commitment and talents.

Rehana Ahmed
May 2004

Preethi Nair

Preethi Nair was the one who sat quietly at the back of the class with unstylish centre-parted hair held together by two clips. In a bid to be put on the 'list' and to be in with the 'in' crowd, she permed it and placed a green bow at the side. The other kids noticed, but not in the way she had hoped.

Somewhere between adolescence and thirty, having got rid of the perm, a transformation took place. She now lives in London, has given up trying to set fashion trends and works as a writer.

Her books include *Gypsy Masala: A Story of Dreams* and *One Hundred Shades of White*.

Jubilee Dreams

Preethi Nair

3 June 2002

My whole family has come round our house to watch the telly. It's not that they don't have tellies; most of them have got satellite dishes and DVD players, but my dad has insisted because it's Golden Jubilee Day and he's really, really into the Queen. My big sister says that in the days before they had videos and that, he used to take photographs of the Queen every time she came on the telly – but these days that's all changing because he says if Prince Charles marries Camilla he won't pay his taxes. I didn't think he paid them anyway.

My aunties and uncles and the rest of the family have all arrived. My big sister, Anita, hasn't got far to travel as she still lives with us. She's twenty-seven. Dad has tried to get her married off for the last ten years, but nobody has taken her off his hands, so their relationship is fraught. Come to think of it, their relationships with most people are fraught.

7

Trevor McDonald is talking about the minimal damage from the effects of the fire at Buckingham Palace, which could have overshadowed the Queen's Jubilee. The camera moves from his face to pictures of firemen outside the palace, and the reporter makes a fleeting comment about Will Young lighting the Queen's fire. Will Young is my hero – he would never do something like that. He is performing at the palace for this huge party, and he's currently number one in the charts with 'Come on, baby, light my fire', so it doesn't make sense – why would he want to start the Queen's fire?

I turn to my big sister and voice my concerns.

'No, you idiot, he didn't do it – it's a double meaning. You won't get it, you're too young.'

'Shhh,' my dad says, trying to catch a glimpse of Her Majesty.

That's what they say about pretty much everything – that I'm too young. Their other favourite line is that life is tough. If it's my dad who says it he'll go on about the days when he would walk ten kilometres to school with no shoes, begging for food. Then he'll go on about how fortunate we are to live in England. That's why he's into the Queen – because he says she gave him a second opportunity by letting him come to England. So you'd think he would be in favour of asylum seekers, but he says most of them are 'bloody scroungers' who are living off his hard-earned money.

I watch the telly closely for more double meanings. Trevor McDonald swiftly moves on to the next news item: tension mounts as England prepare for their World Cup match against Argentina. The camera is on the English coach, Sven-Goran Eriksson, at a news conference.

8

England has drawn one–all against Sweden, and he is not pleased with the team's performance. The camera suddenly cuts from his unhappy face to scenes of an empty Ikea car park. Why did they cut to an empty Ikea car park? Trevor McDonald tries not to look harassed and announces the most important event last: India and Pakistan are about to go to war. I cut from this global historical perspective to our living room at 39 Oakley Drive, Slough – or 'Slog', as my dad pronounces it.

It's an Indian living room, though you wouldn't really know it as we have laminate wood flooring throughout. I think the only things that really give it away are the heavy electric-green curtains and the photographs and statues of incarnated gods everywhere. My dad is shaking his head at the prospect of war. He's worried it will ruin the Queen's celebrations. 'I hope nobody will rain on her parade,' he says. The way he says parade sounds like 'poor head'. Me and my sister look at each other. His concern for world peace touches us.

Maybe he really is deeply concerned about war, but he said what he did because he wanted to use that phrase. Recently he's got into this habit of randomly dropping odd phrases he's picked up into conversations. I think he gets them from his posh customers. He's a cab driver. Sometimes his phrases make no sense; other times it's like playing Countdown and you have to try and unscramble the meaning behind his words within thirty seconds or you lose the gist of the conversation. The other day I heard him telling my mum that they had to keep up with the Jonasis. She agreed. I could tell she didn't know what she was agreeing to, but she pretty much agrees with everything he says. The Jonasis, he insisted, had great cars and houses and holidays, and we had to keep up with them. My sister laughed and said they were called the Joneses.

'It's the Joneses, Dad, JONESES. To keep up with the Joneses.' He threw her a look as if she had just hurled a grenade in his direction.

'When you get married you can tell me then who the Jonasis are, but under my roof I say what I want.'

Trevor McDonald is saying that both the Pakistani troops and the Indian troops are moving nearer to the border. My dad murmurs something offensive about the Pakistanis. He blames them all for any misfortune in his life, but he especially blames generous Mr Khan from the chip shop for ruining his previous business. As they cut to pictures of marching soldiers, I can feel the footsteps treading heavily on my sister's heart. War has so many implications, not just for the world, or even for the Queen's celebrations, but for the microcosm that is our family. My sister is secretly in love with Azhar, Mr Khan's son, and nobody knows.

'Wishing you all a very good evening and a happy Jubilee,' Trevor McDonald says as the news comes to an end. There's a final cut to pictures of the crowds singing 'God Save the Queen'. My dad stands up and joins in; the aunties and uncles begin staring at each other, unsure quite what to do. My dad looks at us, his girls, for choral support, and we make a break for our respective rooms.

After he's finished singing he shouts, 'Bloody children! Give them everything and they still have no respect.' I know what comes next – a speech to our relatives as to why Anita is not married and how I am the one that will make him proud.

*

10

I'm Asha, thirteen and a half, and I go to Wolton Comprehensive. Best features are my eyes. My big sister says that only losers with no good-looking features say that, because you can't really go wrong with eyes – not unless you're cross-eyed like this girl in my class called Elena Kirocia. Worst features are my teeth. My front tooth kind of protrudes, like it wants to escape but the furthest it can get to is the front door. I know that feeling well. I'm desperate to get a brace, but my dad won't let me because he doesn't want 'no bloody dentist ripping me off'. I inform him that it's free for kids on the NHS, and he tells me that nothing is free; that they will rig it so that something will go wrong when I'm eighteen and it will be him or my husband who will have to pay for it.

I've also recently started growing a moustache. Not on purpose or anything – I don't know why it's happened, like I don't know why lots of things happen. My big sister says it's gross and wants me to wax it off, but then the kids at school will know that I've waxed it off. It's like when the boys at school first start shaving, everyone knows. I couldn't take that kind of embarrassment, it's not worth the hair-free look. Besides, I couldn't take the pain of waxing. I'm not really good with pain, not like my mum who's endured years of it.

What else? My hero, like I said before, is Will Young. I bet his dad let him have braces when he was a kid. He's got a lovely smile. At first, my dad wouldn't let me watch the Pop Idol final because he said he didn't want me to get 'fairy-airy' ideas into my head. I was totally gutted and told him I wasn't harbouring any desires to become a singer (I didn't dare mention that I wanted to be a foreign correspondent), but he was having none of it. Then, just

11

before it came on, I tried a different route and said that Will Young was related to the Queen and that the other finalist, Gareth Gates, lived in Bradford and loads of Pakistanis lived there, so he would get the Pakistani vote. He let me watch it and even let me phone in and vote for Will. I don't think I'm devious by nature. I mean, I don't wear long skirts to school and then change into mini ones when I get there. I wouldn't want to do that anyway – my legs are dead skinny. When I wear my chunky shoes, my sister says I look like Olive Oyl off *Popeye*.

I've got lots of posters of Will in my room, but they're all hidden under posters of horses. I don't like horses, but my dad's got a nose like a bloodhound and I had to throw him off the Will Young scent. The only posters I could find in WH Smith that were big enough to cover him were of Shetland ponies and racehorses.

Mum thinks I'm mad about the beasts now, so whenever she gets me stuff it's got some kind of horse print on it. She works at Woolworths, so hasn't got far to go to get any of it, and it makes her feel she's getting a bargain as she uses her staff-discount card. My bag, pencil case, rubber, everything has a horse on it. It's dead embarrassing, but my mum goes without things for herself to buy me stuff, so I don't have the heart to tell her that it's all naff.

Most nights, before I go to bed, I take down all the decoy posters and talk to Will. I tell him about my dreams and how one day I will escape Slog.

This time last week I was talking to Will about school and how desperate I was to be in with Sarah Walker and her gang; how I didn't want to spend break times on my own, hiding from everyone so that they won't see me alone. I told him how everyone thought I was thick just because I didn't say much in class, and how intelligence sometimes comes nicely wrapped in silence. Will understands that kind of talk. I was also talking to him about boys. Not that there's anyone in my year that I like, not even Sanjeev Sekhar who's the most popular guy. And even if I did like him, he wouldn't look twice at me. Anyway, some of the boys in our class made this list, hypothetically pairing up all the boys and girls. They forgot to put my name on it – I didn't even make it against the ugliest guy, Rohin Kapadia. Not that looks are everything, but, I mean, nobody knew that I existed, not even as the ugly one. Just as I was sharing this with Will, my big sister walked in.

'Who are you talking to, Ash?'

'Nobody.'

'Bloody hell, where have all them horses gone? Dad will kill you if he sees him plastered all over the walls,' she said, looking around at Will. 'What have you got him up for anyway? Couldn't you have chosen someone like Ronan?'

'I'm not into Ronan. I love Will.'

'But he's gay. You do know what gay is, don't you?'

How thick was she? Of course I knew what gay was. But that's my big sister all over – likes to think that I'm dumb. And there's no point in trying to show her otherwise, so I just go along with her. It makes her feel better.

'Of course he's gay. He's happy. That's a picture of him winning Pop Idol,' I tell her.

'I mean, how dumb can you get, kid?'

She sat on my bed with me, took out my notebook and began explaining. It was funny watching her explain it with her stupid diagrams. I asked loads of questions to make her feel I was well into it. You could just tell that Anita felt

13

great for imparting some of her wisdom. In those moments of sisterly bonding, I wanted to tell her that I knew about Azhar and her, that I stumbled across them whilst on my solo lunchtime roam and saw them kissing down an alley. She in her British Airways uniform (she works at the check-in desk at Heathrow) and he in his cod-splattered white overalls (he is an IT consultant, but I think that day he was helping his dad out in the chip shop). Taking a break from saying 'Would you like salt and vinegar with that?' and 'Open or closed?', he was unwrapping my sister. It was all getting a bit too much, so I went back to school.

'I know about you and Azhar,' I said as she put away her diagrams.

'You what?' she said, shocked.

'You and Chip Shop Azhar. I know about you, I saw you.'

'Now listen, you ain't seen nothing, I mean it. If you tell anyone, and I mean *anyone*, I'll break both your f****** legs.'

Her command of the English language was quite impressive, and to show she meant what she said, she tore my best poster of Will in half. His head and upper body stayed on the wall looking down at his legs, which were sprawled across my floor. She didn't give me an opportunity to say that I supported her, that once in a while it was good to go against our dad and stand up to authority.

Before I went to sleep, I Blu-tacked the ponies back on the walls and I carried out my ritual of reading all the interview cuttings I had on Will. He always says to believe in your dreams, no matter how remote they seem. Do dreams get heard in Slog? Would he have won Pop Idol if he was living with my dad? He wouldn't have got a brace, that's for sure. What if Dad found out he was gay? I put the light off and went to bed.

The dream I had that night pretty much changed the course of events in my life: Mum, Dad and my sister were sitting like the panel of judges on Pop Idol. The audience was full of the members of my year. Sanjeev Sekhar and Sarah Walker were sitting in the front row with most of my teachers, and Chip Shop Azhar and his dad were just behind them. The lights in the studio were bright. I was on next, auditioning as a foreign correspondent with a piece on the mounting tensions in the disputed region of Kashmir. My legs were like jelly. I took a deep breath, and then I did it. Told them about the reasons for the conflict and the actions taken by both India and Pakistan. As I finished the audience clapped and cheered, and it was over to the judges.

First up was my mum. She made her normal comments: 'Good, *beta*. Did you eat well when you went out there to do filming?' Then it was my sister's turn. Clearly thinking of her own situation, she glanced at Chip Shop Azhar and began to ask me a question about how to cope with knowing inside information without divulging it (she didn't exactly say it in those words, vocabulary not being her strongest point, but that was the gist of it). The moment she made her comments, my dad laid into me. He was shouting that I had been biased, that I hadn't portrayed India favourably, that Pakistanis were the cause of all the trouble; if there was a problem, you had to look no further than the Pakistanis. At that moment, someone began heckling loudly in the audience. The man stood up and said I had done a fantastic job, it was the best piece of reporting

15

he had heard. It was Will. He came down on stage to join me. He argued with my dad, told him what was what, put him in his place and then began singing 'Evergreen'. After everyone cheered, we went backstage together.

'Asha,' he said. 'You were brilliant, just brilliant.'

I looked down, embarrassed. Nobody had ever said I was brilliant before, especially not twice.

'You've got to believe in yourself. If you don't, nobody else will. You've got to give off this vibe that says, "I believe in myself".'

'It's hard, Will,' I replied. 'Life in Slog isn't like it is where you live. I want my dad to be proud of me, not because he thinks I'll be married at eighteen but because he thinks I'm good at what I do. Then I want the teachers to notice I've got a brain and the boys to put me on a list and to be in with Sarah Walker and her gang.'

'Act like you have all those things,' he insisted. 'Believe that anything is possible if you want it enough. Imagine yourself in situations you never thought you would be in, and even if you don't really believe any of it, pretend that you do. You'll see how it all changes. Don't give up, especially when it seems impossible. When things get tough, stick with it. It's just a way of testing that your dreams are really what you want.'

'Is that what you did?' I asked.

He nodded.

'But, Will, this is a dream. It's not reality, and when I wake up you'll be gone.'

'It's not a dream, Asha. What I've said to you is real. It's as real as you want it to be. Tell you what, make a request on the radio this morning before you go to school. Any song of mine, and I'll sing it for you.'

'I've called up Capital hundreds of times. They don't do requests.'

'Believe that this time it will be different,' he insisted.

There were so many questions I wanted to ask him when I had him there, but Will disappeared as my radio alarm went off. I woke up debating whether to wax off my moustache. It would be symbolic, like a change in me; a resolve that things would be different.

My sister was in the shower when I went into her room to get some of her wax strips. It took just a bit of riffling to find them in one of her drawers. As I took them back to my room, I decided it would be best to creep downstairs and make the call whilst everyone was still upstairs. Nervously, I dialled the number. 'Yes, hello, I'd like to make a request for Will Young's "Evergreen". It's for Asha from Slog,' I said to the operator at Capital.

'We don't do requests,' said the woman curtly.

'Asha, is that you? Who are you talking to?' my dad called out to me from the next room. 'Come here. Come see what I've done.'

I rang off suddenly, hoping he hadn't heard me use the phone, and went through to the living room.

'What do you think?' he said, pointing at two pictures he had put up on the wall in preparation for the Jubilee celebrations. The first one was of the Queen in all her regalia – and the second one was frightening. It was a blown-up passport photo of himself taken thirty years ago. He had a bushy moustache, and on the photo was a rubber immigration stamp.

'It was the day I came to England. What do you think?' he repeated. 'Nice, no?' He readjusted it.

17

'It's . . . it's different,' I replied, staring at that scary moustache.

'Different? You don't know anything else to say?'

I told him he looked good and that the moustache did loads for him, thinking that I had to sort out my own.

And then my sister screamed from upstairs. 'Asha, have you been in my bloody room?'

I left my dad to his pictures and walked up the stairs to listen to her ranting. Do you see the distractions I have to put up with, Will? It's all very well talking about dreams and that, but come and live in our house for a week.

Just as I was thinking that, the most amazing thing happened. The alarm on my radio came back on. It sounded so loud. Chris Tarrant was on and he said, 'We don't normally do requests but this is a very special one from Will Young. It's to Asha from Slog. I think that's meant to be Slough, not Slog,' he said.

Honest. That's how it happened. I stopped at the top of the stairs, mesmerized. My sister was shouting and swearing at me, but I couldn't hear any of it. Her lips were moving but no sound came out. And then he sang. He sang 'Evergreen' for me, and it was like . . . like heaven.

There were loads of dancing butterflies in my stomach, transformed from the sluggish caterpillars that used to live there. I couldn't concentrate or sort out my moustache because I was in this really weird state. My fingers kept trembling, so it was impossible to hold the wax strip straight. I managed to do a corner, but I had to leave it there as it killed so much. After that I can't really remember much, except that I must have done the normal stuff like had a shower, got my uniform on and had my cornflakes. This dream thing was true. It really existed. I

18

walked to school feeling like a different person, feeling like I had all the things I'd ever wanted.

It's amazing what a difference a vibe can make. I noticed it first in my stride, which wasn't rigid. My Olive Oyl legs felt like they belonged to the supermodel Naomi Campbell, I carried my horse-print bag as if it was the next fashion accessory, and my protruding tooth seemed unique and special. Kids who never spoke to me before said 'Hi' as I walked through the school gates, and when Miss Bell called out my name at registration I said 'Yes, Miss' so assertively, like I had *arrived*. Everyone turned to stare.

'There's something different about you, Asha,' said Elena Kirocia. Elena was the second most unpopular girl after me, so it was no surprise that she would notice a change like that, it having serious implications for her status. Then she hovered around me, sat next to me in French, saw my awful pony pencil case and tried to strike up a bond by talking about horses. I could have easily found something else to say because I noticed a sticker of Will on her exercise book and she saw me looking at him. 'He's great, isn't he?' she said.

I wanted to tell her – tell her all about the dream and how great he really was. But instead I said, 'Nah, I'm into Eminem.' A week ago, I would have jumped at the chance to speak to Elena, but now things were different, I didn't want second best. It was time to go for the big time: for Sarah Walker and her gang.

Sarah Walker wore her tie around her waist, and the teachers couldn't say anything because the most important thing was to have it on. Maria, Kalpana, Seema all followed. These were the key members of her gang who she would play off against each other. It was meant to be a

19

privilege and an honour to sit next to her, and I knew that soon I would be there; not rotating like the others did, but permanently sitting next to her, chatting away with my tie around my waist, flicking my hair like she did. I had to play it cool, though, think strategically. People can smell desperation a mile off; this is what my big sister always says to me.

We had double-English and I went for the kill, answering all of Mr Ivy's questions as if Will was there in the audience, egging me on. I didn't do it in a know-it-all way, but sort of jokily, and all the other kids started to laugh. Sarah and her gang turned to stare.

After English, Elena leeched on to me, I couldn't get rid of her. Then Kalpana and Seema came to talk. I was desperate to respond, but I ignored them. It was the boss I wanted to see, not the sidekicks. By lunchtime, she herself approached me.

'Heard you're into Eminem. That right?' probed waist-tied Sarah Walker.

And before I had a chance to say that rap wasn't real music, not like the stuff Will did, it came flying out of my mouth: 'I'm a Slim Shady.' I even did this horrific dance move.

She laughed, then the rest of the gang laughed.

'You're quite funny, really. It's Ash, isn't it?'

I couldn't believe it. She said I was funny and she knew my name. I was bursting with excitement. Surely next would be an invitation to sit with her, join them for lunch – but then I saw her expression. Elena was standing next to me. Sarah Walker's eyes darted towards her as if to say 'lose the hanger-on or there's no deal'.

Then I did something awful. I don't think I'm spiteful

deep down, but this was a rare opportunity; this was the moment I had been waiting for. 'Haven't you got to go to Specsavers or something, Elena?'

The girls had roared with laughter and that was the moment I was invited into Sarah Walker's gang. That's how I came to hang out with them the whole of last week and how some of the boys noticed me and told Sanjeev to put me on the list – and from then on I was on a roll, answering questions in class and making everyone laugh.

It's weird, but it doesn't feel like I thought it would, Will. I keep telling myself it's the best feeling ever to be with all of them, though. I got so carried away that I invited Sarah Walker and the gang around for one of the Jubilee holidays. They're coming tomorrow. Mum, Dad and my sister will be at work, thank God, and I thought we could chill up here in my room. Dad's sitting downstairs singing 'God Save the Queen' to the relatives, and I've left him to it so I can talk to you, Will, to explain why I'm doing this, why I am taking you down. I want you to know that I'm so very sorry and deep down it's not what I feel. But I hope you'll understand. I have to go for my dream.

The horse posters are coming down. I fold up all the posters of Will and put them in my bottom drawer. I go into my WH Smith bag and take out posters of Eminem, stick him everywhere, and put the horse posters back on top.

My dad is shouting for us: 'Anita, Asha, bloody get down these stairs and help Mummy. These girls do nothing,' he says to my relatives.

5 June 2002

That night, I didn't read the interviews on Will. I went to sleep thinking I should be feeling happy, that the culmination of my dreams would arrive within twenty-four hours. But as I switched off the light I felt strangely alone.

I got up early just to make sure everyone would be safely at work, doing their overtime. They're like that my family; even if there's something dead important like a wedding or a funeral on an overtime day, they go for overtime every time, cos 'money don't grow from the trees', as my dad says.

'Why are you up so early?' my sister asked.

'I'm going to the library,' I replied, looking in my dad's direction, 'to do some studying.'

'Good. Good girl,' he said, glaring back at my sister. 'At least one of you can do something good.'

'So everyone's at work then today?' I enquired, just to make sure.

'Bloody looks like it,' my sister shouted. 'We can't all sit and do nothing or talk to posters.'

My mum kissed me as she was leaving and told me that there were rotis with egg curry in the fridge for my lunch, and to eat well. I'd throw that over the fence so that there'd be no trace that I hadn't eaten at home. Me and the gang would probably go and hang out in McDonald's.

By eight o'clock they had all left and I went up to take the horse posters down again. In four hours' time, Sarah Walker would be here, in my house. I couldn't believe it. I had a shower, thought carefully about what to wear, had my breakfast and watched *This Morning* to kill time – but I couldn't concentrate. This meeting, here in my house, was important; it would consolidate my status as gang member and, hopefully, it would go so well that I wouldn't have to do the rotation thing.

The bell rang. It was them.

Seema hadn't come, but the other three stood on the doorstep, with cut-off jeans, crop tops and belly-button rings. I felt stupid in my baggy T-shirt and leggings.

'You wanna get yours done, Ash,' Sarah said as my eyes went to their midriffs.

'Yeah, I was thinking about it,' I lied, imagining my dad's horrified face. 'Come in,' I said, and led them into the sitting room.

'Yous lot into this elephant thing, then,' Sarah commented as she looked at the numerous statues. 'Bloody hell, who's that?' She stopped at the framed picture of my dad.

'Some old relative,' I said, trying to distract her.

There was this spooky silence. I read those silences well, them being common between Mum and Dad. Dad wanting Mum to come up with something interesting and exciting besides roti and egg curry . . . and Mum surprising him with roti and egg curry. Dad wanting Mum to change her centre-parted hair . . . and Mum surprising him with centre-parted hair. The gang looked at each other and silence bombarded the room. Anticipation mounted as to what my party piece would be.

'I've got Eminem's new CD if you guys want to come up and listen,' I said eagerly. It wasn't really mine; I had borrowed it from my big sister.

'Yeah, awight. We'll just have a fag first,' Sarah Walker said as she pulled out a cigarette packet.

Fag, fag, I thought, terrified. Imagining my dad's bloodhound nose, I jumped up and said, 'It's much nicer out in the garden.' So they followed me out.

'Bit overgrown, innit?' said Kalpana as she looked around at the forest that was our garden.

Sarah lit up and I got ready to pretend I had smoked a thousand cigarettes. But when the cigarette came round to me I coughed as I swallowed the smoke.

'You'll get used to it,' Maria said. 'At first I didn't like it, but then Sarah taught me how to inhale properly.' She looked in Sarah's direction. No doubt that comment would earn her prime position next to Sarah for a week or so. Kalpana, sensing the competition, felt she had to do something to beat the Cigarette Queen's comments, so she blew an almost perfect circle with her smoke. Unfortunately it landed in Sarah Walker's airspace. The look Kalpana got off Sarah Walker confirmed she was out of prime position for the next couple of weeks. I needed to know where Seema was in the running to work out what kind of chance I stood.

'Where's Seems?' I enquired.

'Out with Sanjeev,' Sarah said, clearly pissed off.

So, I thought, there was only one person to beat off and surely it wouldn't be that hard.

Kalpana tried to retrieve her position by saying that Sanjeev wasn't that fit anyway, and that the best guy was Simon Hill and anyone could see how much he fancied Sarah.

As we were standing in the garden, talking about boys and that, I thought I heard the door go.

'Who's that?' Sarah Walker asked.

My heart pounded. My life wouldn't be worth living if Bloodhound-Nose Dad came back. Then, I heard my sister's giggle.

'Did you hear someone?' Chip Shop Azhar asked her.

'Nah, Azhar, no one's in. Let's go upstairs.'

'Oh, baby,' he said. 'Oh, baby . . . oh, baby.' (He didn't have an extensive vocabulary either.)

From then on it was like some horror film I didn't want to be in. I had to find a way of getting the gang out of the house, but as Anita and Chip Shop Azhar climbed the stairs Sarah Walker said, 'Shall we listen to the main man, then?' All I could think of when she said that was Chip Shop Azhar making weird sounds as he touched my sister.

I couldn't explain it to them; they wouldn't understand if I told them that my sister would break my legs if she found us there listening to the main man. But that number-one spot sitting next to Sarah Walker was so near. I couldn't give it up.

So, with the full knowledge that I was risking my life, I led them upstairs to my room.

'Shhh,' I heard my sister say to Chip Shop Azhar.

'It's only me,' I shouted, 'with a few friends. We're just going to listen to some music.' Her music. But, amazingly, she said nothing and shouted no obscenities. Maybe she was tied up with other things.

I quickly got them all into my room. They were well impressed with my posters, but just as I put the CD track on and got down with some moves, the door knob of my room turned.

My dream turned into a nightmare: my dad was standing there. Normally he takes a packed lunch to work, but he had obviously decided to come home for lunch, thinking he might catch a glimpse of the Queen's carnival 'poor head' on telly.

It's difficult for me to relive those moments of him staring in amazement at the belly buttons, the posters of

Eminem, me with his and my mum's jewellery on my hands (so I could get into the rapper's role). He switched off the CD player, and in the silence that followed my sister and the main man could be heard loud and clear, Chip Shop Azhar shouting 'Oh, baby'. My dad stormed into her room, finding my sister unwrapped in Chip Shop Azhar's arms. Then he went ballistic, shouting and swearing, calling us all sorts, and saying we had ruined him. Sarah Walker told him not to overreact, cos it wasn't like he was my dad or anything – he was just some old relative. He turned towards her and called her a 'cheap belly-button girl' and accused her of being the one behind all of this. She called him a 'bloody lunatic' and he told her to 'bloody get out of my house – and take your "robber music" or whatever it is with you'. She left with her gang, calling him a 'loser'. Then he said he'd deal with me later and went to sort out Chip Shop Azhar and my sister.

That's where I'm up to, Eminem. That's what you get from following a stupid Will Young dream, giving off a different vibe. I'm in the depths of despair and there's no one there for me, least of all you, Eminem, cos I was never into you in the first place. My sister has left home. My dad won't speak to me, my mum's not supposed to speak to me and Sarah and her gang will never speak to me again. Next week I have to go back to school, and they'll crucify me.

Defeated, I crawl into bed.

The radio alarm goes off at 4:00 a.m., and his voice comes on smooth, sad but confident. I am half asleep and so maybe I hear what I want to hear. Will sings 'Ain't no sunshine when she's gone', and I hear that he's singing it for

Asha. I start to cry. I cry and cry because he hasn't really left me, he's always been there; even when I left, he was still there. I ask him why. Why is following a dream so hard? Why was it nothing like I had expected? I cry until there are no more tears and my breath goes all funny. As I put my head back on the pillow, the answer comes back to me: 'When things get tough, stick with it. It's just a way of testing that your dreams are really what you want.'

'Thank you, Will, thank you.' I lie awake thinking about things. I want my family back together, for Dad not to be disappointed in us, to have friends that I enjoy being around and whom I can be myself with.

4 June 2003

It was hard going back to school after that. I waxed off my moustache as I thought I had nothing to lose anyway. Sarah Walker and her gang gave me hell, and so did the rest of my class. Everyone except Elena. I got through it, knowing that it would all get better – that I had to just hold on and believe it would. Things did change; I've learned that if you want them to enough, they do.

My dad didn't speak to my sister for months, but broke down when he accidentally saw her. He talks to her now and made some emotional speech about how hard it must have been for the Queen to finally come to accept Camilla. He's trying his best to get on with both Chip Shop Azhar and Mr Khan, but we can't really expect too much there.

I don't have to hide my posters of Will any more either, because I've explained to my dad that it's important to have role models – and I gave him Will's CV, adding that he was closely related to the Queen and therefore royalty. He agreed it was better to have royalty as a role model than 'the robber'. My mum's even stopped getting me stuff with horses on, but she's still got a centre parting and surprises us with roti and egg curry every day. What else? I've come top in my class and I'm proud of it, and, most importantly, I've got this brilliant, brilliant best friend called Elena, and we do loads together. We've just found out we've been shortlisted to be newshounds on *Newsround*.

If I make it on *Newsround* I'll have to have straight teeth, but I've not quite sorted out the brace situation. I'm currently doing research to see if any of the royal family had them fitted. I mean the Queen must have had it done. Her teeth are dead straight; they have to be cos that's her job – to smile at everyone, even when they give her gifts she's not ever going to use. I wonder if the Queen ever dreams for something, gets it and then finds out it's not really what she wants.

But now I do know what you mean, Will. Sometimes things don't work out as you expect, sometimes what you really think you want isn't what's best for you. In which case, something else always comes along.

Romesh Gunesekera

R omesh Gunesekera was born in Sri Lanka and lived in several countries before moving to Britain. He always wanted to be a writer and started out on a tightrope: reading, working at various jobs, discovering the world and dreaming up stories.

He has always been keen on short stories, and his first book, *Monkfish Moon*, has nine of them. He also writes poems, which have been published in various anthologies, including some for very young readers. His first novel, *Reef*, was a finalist for the 1994 Booker Prize as well as the Guardian Fiction Prize, and his next book, *The Sandglass*, received the first BBC Asia Award for Achievement in Writing & Literature in 1998. His most recent novel is *Heaven's Edge*.

To find out more, or to contact Romesh Gunesekera, go to his website: www.romeshgunesekera.com

Tightrope

Romesh Gunesekera

1

'**O**scar! Come and eat.'

My mother's voice was always sharp. The words snagged on the net curtains hung out to dry on the landing. I ignored them. They were old words. I'd heard them before. Every day for as long as I could remember. They were the sounds of time passing: like the buses on the road, or water in the pipes, the whine of a washing machine stuck in a rut.

'Oscar, *food*.'

She and Lenny, my younger brother, would be picking at chicken bones, leftover rice, curried vegetables that had been crushed into one another; eating loudly and clucking from the kitchen to the back extension until they lost the point of it all. Even on a Sunday that my father was at home, it was not much different. They'd congregate in one place then, but still munch mindlessly to themselves and get lost in shopping lists, lottery grunts or yesterday's junk mail. Farmyard feeders in suburban gear, that's what they were.

I picked up the remote and pressed the red button. The screen in the corner flared with a zing and I felt sucked in. Rubbery. I liked that. But the face on the screen, I didn't like. With my thumb I pressed the channel-up button several times, then held it down like an accelerator and watched half a dozen screen faces flash by. I liked that too. The idea that there were so many out there which I could ignore: turn off. Not you, not you, not you.

'Oscar, if you're not eating I'll put the rice in the fridge. You take what you want. I have to go in ten minutes to drop Lenny.'

Thank you, I replied politely in my mind. You don't have to say it as long as you've thought it. I didn't want food just then. My hunger was for something more . . . *intangible*, like fleeting images that disappeared – phantom fish in a pool, suggesting possibilities but never becoming solid, heavy, cooked and dead.

'Oscar? You must eat something. And remember, we go back to the hospital at six. Be ready.'

'OK.'

I bit my lip too late. The OK had slipped out. It always makes me cross to realize I have so little control. The one word hung in the room, accusing me of a weak will. A loose mouth. Two syllables. Two silly bells. My father would not have given in so easily. But then I pictured him, sunk in his hospital bed, giving in. I quickly pressed the remote again. The TV blinked. A grey ghost faded, wordlessly, into the screen.

2

Sparrow told me the other day that willpower was what made humans human. 'No willpower, no nothing.'

I'd never considered that. We were in my room, thinking. Recently we'd both discovered how wild this could be.

'Think about it. If you have no will, you live like a dog. You just react.'

'But *you* react. You react all the time.' I was not going to just sit back and swallow any old tripe he threw up in the air. No way.

Sparrow screwed up his face until his lips and eyes disappeared into thin folds of skin. His puckered head shifted back and relocated in the depths of his shoulders. He had no neck left. 'That's cos I want to react. If I didn't want to, I could hold back. Not react or react – it's my choice. That's willpower. Real power.'

'Anyway, a dog knows stuff too. They choose too.' I wasn't very happy with his line of discrimination. I like dogs. A dog's life, I think, could be paradise. Wordless. Real. Imagine what you would see as a dog. Everything would be from a lower altitude. Lower even than Lenny. Everything big would be taller and longer. Wilder and weirder.

Sparrow claimed that dogs don't even see in colour, but how would he know? How would anyone but a dog really know? Anyway, maybe they smell and hear colour instead. They remember things – so, what lights up in their heads then? What would my red socks be like? Rina's blue-glass bangles? Imagine taste instead of colour. Texture. Sound. It could be OK, as a life.

Sparrow pulled his legs into a lotus position, withdrawing.

'So, what are you doing now?' I asked. I had learned to be wary with him.

'Waiting.'

'For what?'

'The right time.'

Now that, I thought, was something neat. I was also waiting for the right time. But until Sparrow said it, I had never realized it. I hadn't thought that I too could be waiting for a sense of willpower to grow in me and tell me what to do. Tell me what I wanted, besides the obvious stuff that everybody wanted. Or said they wanted.

Sparrow talked rubbish most of the time, but there was something in what he said about willpower and waiting that stuck, like a string of celery between my teeth. It made me think about Sparrow in a different way. Sometimes he said exactly the words you needed, almost by accident. Come to think of it, he was a celery stick himself. Especially with his shabby cords and wilted hair.

Sparrow said he had deep lines, like crevices, running down the soles of his feet. 'You have lines like that?' he asked slyly.

'I dunno,' I said.

'Let's see.'

'I don't want you looking at my feet.'

'They tell the future, you know, those lines.'

'That's on your palm, you idiot.' I was not going to be tricked so easily.

'This is something else. A special thing my sister taught me.'

Sparrow's sister was clever. She carried a lot of knowledge, easily. I was often damaged just by the thought of her.

'You can read them?'

Sparrow nodded.

'OK then,' I said, and peeled off my socks. There were things I wanted to know. About myself. The past. The future. Sparrow's big sister. I was in that kind of a mood.

Sparrow peered forward and made a sound with his tongue like something was gurgling down a plughole. 'Too faint. Those are way too faint.'

I twisted my foot upwards to check for myself. I could make out a few spidery wrinkles but most of the skin looked like melted candle wax. Some patches were speckled with black grime and glossed over like a dirty gym floor. The arch of the foot seemed very pale and seriously deformed.

'You have to rub lemon juice for those lines to really show up.'

'Rubbish.'

Sparrow shrugged.

I hobbled over to the bathroom to wash my feet instead. While I was rinsing them in the bath, Sparrow shouted out that he had to go. He left.

When I returned I couldn't find my socks anywhere. I didn't mind at first. It's not unusual not to be able to find things in here. The universe, they say, is a mystery. So's my room. I had no reason to suspect anything.

3

On Channel Four, a goldfish was pumping hard, the heart beating ultra-fast. It looked like it couldn't go on much longer. I used my thumb for the mute button. I had read in *The Book of Deeper Secrets* that every heart has a number. A number of beats it will beat no matter what. Nothing can stop the number; nothing can extend it. You could cross a desert without water if you hadn't reached the last number. You could swim the Atlantic, underwater, if you had enough beats. Basically, you survive anything if you are meant to. I liked the idea. So very sub-zero.

My father, propped up in his sickbed, was not impressed when I mentioned what I'd discovered. He said that such stories were dangerous nonsense. The heart is an organ, not a clock. He broke the word to emphasize it. *Ker-lock*. 'You don't wind it up.'

But hey, Dad, hello? Nobody winds clocks any more.

4

TV muted, I rolled over to the window. Years of moisture had collected on the lower edges making them sag and turn black with mildew. Outside, the sky looked as if it was made of metal. The clouds were low enough to suck, like stage-smoke. A few autumn crocuses spiked the grass. A blackbird killed a worm. A squirrel slipped off a slimy tree.

The back of my head hurt. My neck. Actually my whole body, right down to my feet. A meltdown. It started yesterday and has been gathering speed ever since.

It was Rina's fault. She said something really stupid yesterday and put me completely off track. I was just beginning to like her, and was hoping she wouldn't say something stupid – but then she did.

She said that she knew all about my problem. Her face widened with girlie concern.

'Like what?'

'Like I know you have this . . . disease.'

I just stared at her. 'Oh, yeah?'

'Sparrow told me it affects your skin. Something to do with your toes. And that you have to keep them always covered with special socks and that you have to go to a hospital now for treatment . . .'

'He's an idiot.'

'But I saw you going to the hospital this morning, from the bus.'

'Why do you listen to that birdbrain? He's an idiot.' I was getting angrier by her every word. Even *bus* made me almost flip. I had been to see my father in hospital. It was a serious thing.

'I thought he's your friend.'

'*You* are an idiot.'

I shouldn't have said it. You can't call a girl an idiot and expect her to feel good about it.

5

I reckon we all actually live on separate planets, and that these planets seem to share the same space only to fool us. People see each other as if they are in the same place, but there is a glass bubble around each of us. We are like goldfish in separate bowls right next to each other. And the bowls are expandable. When you swim up against the edge, it moves out, so you never realize it is there. You swim and you swim and you swim, but you can never get there. Other people come close and gulp in your face, but you can't reach them. Gulp, gulp, gulp. Sink.

I didn't know what I really felt about Rina. Never mind her, I didn't even know what I felt about Sparrow. When I woke up this morning I realized Sparrow must have sneaked away my red socks after his rubbish about sole lines. But why? What kind of an animal would steal a pair of socks. Unwashed. Practically off my feet. A CD, I could understand. A mobile. Trainers, OK. But socks . . . is so, so unbelievably sad.

6

I heard the front door shut. My mother had learned to give up on goodbyes with me. I never answered. It was a point of principle. I learned it from my father.

The sudden emptiness of the house seemed to go straight to my stomach and drew me to the kitchen. I realized I did need sustenance.

When I entered, the refrigerator stopped humming as if it had sensed my presence. I opened it and stood in the glow of the milk light, waiting for the invisible intergalactic snowman inside to tell me the truth about myself. That what I needed was a sandwich. Ham, I heard it sigh. I wanted ham. Someone had tried to hide the ham by putting an economy-pack of low-fat yogurt on top. But no chance: five pink, vacuum-packed, honey-roasted slices peeped out, glistening with that green shine that suggests both a kind of greedy beauty and some exotic illness. I wanted ham in white bread – thick sliced – with loads of yellow butter. Nobody would see me make my sandwich, and nobody would see me eat it. Not my mother, not my father, not Lenny. The pleasure would be mine and mine alone.

I kicked the fridge door shut and put the packet on the table. A pile of sliced bread was leaning precariously against the toaster in an open polythene bag. In our house nobody else seemed to close anything, except their minds. I took out two slices and placed them on a chopping board.

They looked astonishing, like . . . well, just like two slices of white bread on a chopping board: flat, white, absorbent, patient, with brown edges that perfectly mirrored each other. I liked the way the edges looked a little warped on the top and curled out in a small lip at the corner.

I spread a huge blob of butter on one slice. Why is it yellow, if milk is so white? What is colour, anyway? Light waves sinking and bouncing, the meaning entirely dependent on our eyes? If there were no eyes in the world, would there be colour? Would roses be red? And ham pink? Would pigment still be pigment, or would it be a state of pork? And my hand. What colour would it be, really?

I ran my thumb around the plastic shell of the packet of ham, feeling for the flap with which to peel the top off. When I found it, I pulled like tomorrow had definitely been postponed forever. No deal. I pulled again, and pulled the packet right out of my other hand. The ham stayed sealed. I grabbed a knife off the draining board and stabbed it. The packet went pop. The plastic flopped. I cut open the cover and teased out a couple of slices with the tip of the knife. They quivered a moment in the kitchen air before tumbling into the sink. 'Ham!' I cussed out aloud.

Sparrow's favourite cuss was pig head.

'Shouldn't it be pig-headed?' I asked him once, a little bookishly.

'Two syllables. Double punch.'

'What about fat face, then?'

'That's good too. But it's kind of literal. You have to think pig.' He laughed. 'Lateral. *Big*.'

I fished out the ham from the sink and slammed it on to the buttered bread. Slapped the other slice on top and

stuffed it all in my mouth. *Ham*. That's the word I would go
for. Ham you too, Sparrow. Damn sock thief.

7

Back on the sofa – belly filled – I figured the real trouble
with Sparrow was that he didn't value friendship. He didn't
care who his friends were. All he seemed to want was an
audience. He liked to say things and he wanted someone to
hear him; he liked to do things to provoke a reaction. It
could be from anyone. It didn't seem to matter to him.
Sparrow simply used people like they were lumps of clay.
He seemed to want only to create an impression, to make a
mark. Why? I couldn't understand this desire to have an
effect on somebody, if that somebody could be anybody.

Sparrow was not the only one. Even my mother seemed
to have this craving to make an impression on the anony-
mous. Dressing up, for example, whenever she stepped out
of the house, like she was about to be whisked away to
heaven. Or take chat-show clowns, or pop stars on TV,
strutting about with their snouts twitching in the air, posing
for people they would never ever know. People they
couldn't even be sure existed. What was the point? At least
with Sparrow there was some attachment to reality. At least
he wanted some contact, even if he also wanted control. I
didn't mind that. I could fight back. The problem was that
Sparrow just didn't care *who* the other person was.

But despite that, there was something I liked about him.
I guess it was because, unlike all those other people
prancing about in the dark, on TV, or on the street,
Sparrow was interested in something outside himself. From
that, I felt, something meaningful could be made. I wanted

to tell Sparrow about this possibility, but didn't know how to begin. It was all too vague. Just an idea that we could be on the verge of something new. A different kind of existence created out of astral DNA that would connect us all to one cosmic brain, which was the universe. I wanted to tell him that with a little bit of thinking we might work out that the time was now and that the waiting was over. That we already knew who we were and what we wanted. That we knew who our friends were. I imagined the sounds coming out of my mouth and falling apart, senselessly. 'What?' he'd spit with such contempt that I cringed even as I thought of it. It made me wish people could understand each other instantly. Wordlessly.

That is why I like the TV mute. The reason I don't usually say everything I want to.

Maybe I was already becoming like my father. He too used to hardly ever speak. He was always thinking – or seemed to be – but he didn't like to talk much. As though he thought that by putting it into words he might destroy the thing he was trying to describe.

Until, that is, yesterday at the hospital.

8

When we visited him yesterday Dad asked me to wait behind while the others went to find a vase for the flowers we'd brought. 'Listen, son, what keeps us apart sometimes is what keeps us together,' he said when we were alone.

'What do you mean?' I was mystified.

'You are young.'

'Yeah, Dad. Whatever.'

He rubbed at a bit of white stubble on his chin, filling the space between us with a deafening rasp. 'Listen, you need to understand that your mother is under a lot of strain. I guess we both have been.'

I stared at him as if I was seeing him for the first time in ages. He looked like a stranger in the ward. He was going bald on top and his skin had been sandpapered and smeared with ash. His eyes were bloodshot and there were heavy wrinkles like curtains gathered at the edges. Something had gone wrong with his whole shape. He had never looked like this before. He had always had neat black hair, sharp clean eyes and warm brown skin. His moustache was never lopsided. There had never been any grey in it. I could remember how I used to touch it to feel the thick, precise bristles. He used to be so much taller than me.

He coughed into his hand and cleared his throat. 'It hasn't been easy. I know I am not at home much these days, but accounts are not like they used to be. I have to do the job the way they want me to, otherwise I'd lose everything.' He hesitated and glanced around the room. 'But your mother doesn't always appreciate how difficult it is, you know?'

I didn't know what there was to appreciate so much in the accounts department. His difficulties did not seem to be mine – yesterday. Silently, I studied the bunch of flowers lying on the bedside table. I didn't know what else to do. The waxy yellow paper was crumpled where she had clutched the stems. When I looked back at him, his eyes wobbled a little as though the blood in them was turning.

'You find out you can't always remember everything – where you started and where you are heading – when you are trying to keep everything balanced. Like on a tightrope, you know?'

'Tightrope?'

He gazed at me as if he was trying to focus down an unfamiliar road. 'You see, son, you discover life becomes a little bit like a . . .' He paused, as though he thought he ought to weigh the word in his mouth before letting it out again.

'What exactly are you trying to say?' I reckoned it was the drugs they must have given him. Serious clinical drugs.

His mouth opened again. I could see his lips were dry. There was a small blister at one corner and some thin, almost transparent, skin was peeling. I could hear air coming out of his mouth in small puffs. The panting became quieter as though some old-fashioned steam train was moving away from us into another world. He didn't say anything more for a while. Then he smiled weakly. 'Nothing. Nothing you don't already know, I guess, son.'

But all I knew was that the other day, while I was surfing off the sofa after school, he had suffered a severe chest pain and been rushed to hospital from his office. Apparently it was a mild heart attack. Nothing to worry about, I was told later, but he was going to be kept in hospital for a couple of days. OK. I had swallowed hard, pretending along with everyone else that it was not a real complaint. But, then, what was his body trying to say?

I could not understand how he had let himself go like that. Didn't he know how to take care of himself? Don't you learn that sort of thing as you grow older? That money isn't everything. That life isn't a circus. That you have to tend to things around you, look after yourself. That you can't just brood for years like a disgruntled foreigner and then, when you are bald and fat and tired, have a heart attack and start talking in ringside metaphors about life.

My father was an accountant who had lost count, and yet he was now acting like some high-wire geezer in a collapsed tent.

Or was it me? Was I the one who was putting those words in his mouth?

Maybe it was really my mother's fault. Some sort of poetic justice for the way she sometimes, after one too many of her little Bell's, accused him of having no heart. He'd turn up the TV then and gulp down his own double Scotch, double fast. He'd watch any crap to escape a difficult conversation.

Maybe that was why she seemed so awkward with the flowers. Even so, I was glad when she came back down the ward with Lenny, carrying a big plastic jug full of hospital water.

9

The doorbell rang. I went to the front door and looked through the peephole.

'Oink, oink. Come on. Let's go. Rina's waiting at Blockbuster's.' Sparrow pressed the doorbell again, harder.

'OK, OK.' I unlocked the door. But did I want to see Rina ever again? What would I say now? What would she? And why was it that Sparrow was always there? I could see the three of us huddled together in front of a bunch of insane, overrated videos trying to agree on a film none of us really cared for. Would she be between Sparrow and me, or was I going to be the one in the middle? Or would it be Sparrow? Who was keeping whom apart? Was it the same one who was bringing us together?

I saw my father's grey face break into a fragile smile again.

'Come on.' Sparrow pulled my arm.

I shook him off. 'Wait, you've got my socks.'

'What?'

'You took them.'

'*Noh*.' Sparrow's voice went low, as though he was really saying, *What-you-have-lost-is-your-brain-dork*.

'What did you say to Rina about me?'

'You?'

'My feet.' I wanted to get a grip. I wanted my socks. I wanted more. Lots more.

Then I caught his eye and we both cracked up. I don't know why I laughed. I didn't care. For a brief moment, before my life changed from a trampoline to a tightrope, I didn't need words. Something miraculous rushed up my spine, linking each knot to the other, whistling and chortling and making me reel, freewheel, and feel everything was somehow going to be all right. That everything *was* all right. I was laughing. I couldn't stop laughing. It just burst out. I forgot all that had happened before. I forgot to worry about what might happen next. I forgot my father, my mother, my brother and me. I hopped on the thin bridge of the cold doorstep just laughing and laughing, and Sparrow laughed with me.

When we finally stopped, out of breath, he pulled a pair of red socks out of his back pocket and threw them in my face. 'Come on, hurry up. She's waiting for you, pig head.'

I slipped them on quickly, and then my trainers. My time had come. I knew it. I knew what to do. I'd see her, I'd go to the hospital. I'll do everything. I'll find a way – my own way – faster than my dad had ever even dreamed of.

In two minutes I was out, walking light on a rope stretched tight to infinity.

Farrukh Dhondy

Farrukh Dhondy was born in India and went to school and college in a town which used to be called Poona, but which has changed its name to Pune. He won an Indian scholarship to Cambridge University and left India for the first time at the age of nineteen to come to England. After he'd finished with universities, he stayed in England for all the usual reasons – love, money, a job, the possibility of an audience for his writing.

Having taught English in schools in London for a few years, he quit. He had published a few books by then and was writing plays and series for television. He then got a job in TV as a commissioning editor for Channel Four, choosing the programmes that would be produced and screened. But after doing this for twelve years he wanted to be a full-time writer again.

Farrukh's latest book for young adults is called *Run*, and he is currently writing film scripts for Bollywood.

Yellow Dog

Farrukh Dhondy

Tara noticed that her grandfather was getting very thin. The poor old man had to grab his trousers every now and then and pull them up as they slipped off his waist and rested on his sharp hip bones. The legs of his trousers would get crumpled and gather round his ankles. Sometimes, when he didn't have a hand free, this trick with his trousers became very awkward and he'd try and grip them with his elbows to stop them falling off him altogether.

Tara noticed all this, but she would never dare to initiate a conversation on falling trousers or anything about his appearance. It was obviously worrying the old man. Three or four times he said he would buy a good leather belt when he could save enough money. He said he wouldn't make a sash out of old clothes and tie it round his waist as tramps and beggars did, because that was too undignified.

Tara had shifted the button on his trousers to the right twice already, trying to make them tighter. She was quite handy with a needle and thread. She had to be, because she lived alone with her grandfather in Ghasleyt Gali,

Kerosene Alley, in a small town miles away from the big city of Mumbai in India. There was no one else to do their stitching and patching.

Their little winding street was called Ghasleyt Gali because at either end there were shops that sold oil from large metal drums. The goats that belonged to the houses of the alley could always be identified when they wandered off by the strong scent of kerosene that came from their coats. Everything in the alley and in their house reeked of it. The smell got into the food, into the clothes, into the bed. But Tara had been there since she was a child and didn't notice it.

It would never have occurred to Tara to ask why they lived there, but her grandfather told the story to every visitor they ever had – though they rarely had visitors. He said they had always lived there. His father had been the man who lit the street lamps in the town when they still burned kerosene oil. When he started work he did the same, but then electricity arrived. That was progress, modern times. The lamps in the streets of the town were converted. Poles were erected, wires were connected and he was taught a new trade. Tara's grandad had proudly become the man who had the job of cleaning the shades and changing the bulbs of the street lamps. At first it was only one street and then slowly the electrification spread like a spider's web.

But now that he was old, he had been demoted. He was now the man who held the ladder of a younger man, who polished the lamps and changed the bulbs.

Tara was twelve. This was the first year that she had been allowed by her grandad to bring some money into their house by delivering cans of kerosene for the oil shops. The oil didn't go into street lamps now: it was sold as fuel for stoves to all the houses in the neighbourhood. She handed over most of her earnings to her grandad, but secretly kept some back. She was saving it to buy him something, and as Diwali approached she thought she had enough to buy her grandad a beautiful leather belt, with a long and subtle silver buckle. Then he could hold his trousers and head up high.

Her plan seemed to be working. The evening before Diwali, before her grandad returned from work, she went to the Main Street, to the one big shop which sold ready-made clothing, and bought the belt she had seen in the window. It cost her all the money she had saved, but it was worth it. The salesman unrolled it and asked Tara to hold it and to feel the softness of the leather. Tara did as she was told, even though she was thinking she wouldn't know hard leather from soft.

It was getting dark as she hurried back home with the black belt in a plastic bag. The streets were lit for Diwali, the festival of lights. Little oil lamps – small palms of red-clay pottery with string wicks – burned on the window ledges and on the stone steps of all the houses. Tara was nearly home when she ran into a crowd of people who had gathered close to where Ghasleyt Gali was wedged between the houses of the Main Street. Traffic had stopped. There were rickshaws, cycles and a lot of shouting from the street urchins, who formed most of the excited crowd.

As Tara pushed her way through the crowd she heard a man shouting, 'Get out of the way. Oi, you, shift to side.'

Tara saw a man with a gun. The crowd was closing around him, staring at him. He pressed his rifle to his shoulder and then lowered it several times. People shuffled and moved as he pointed it this way and that.

51

'Kick it,' the urchins were shouting, and Tara saw that they were referring to a little yellow dog with matted hair who was trying his best to pass through the legs of the crowd and run away. The urchins wouldn't let him escape.

'Get out of way, or you die of bullets or bitings. This is yellow cocker, most biter,' the man shouted, and raised his gun to his shoulder, taking aim at the dog.

The crowd of boys rapidly parted, and the dog made a run for it. The man with the rifle ran after him, paused and took a shot. The sound of the rifle rang out: 'Tok!'

As Tara watched, the dog ran under the back wheel of a motorcycle rickshaw and let out a piercing yelp.

The crowd didn't know whether the dog was crying because he had been hit by the bullet or crushed under the wheels of the rickshaw. They weren't to find out. In a yellow streak, the dog disappeared into Ghasleyt Gali. The gunman followed, and behind him went the crowd of jeering urchins. Tara followed them.

The gunman slowed down as he entered the alley. He was wearing an olive-green army hat with its brim shadowing his eyes. Below that he wore a long shirt flowing to his knees and tight khaki trousers, Indian style, which bunched up at his ankles. He wore large leather slippers on his feet. He was irritated with the urchins, and he turned and waved the muzzle of his rifle at them.

'You bastards, you see the fellow is absconding,' he said. Then he cursed them and the mothers who had brought them into the world in Urdu, and pretended to aim his gun at them.

The boys dashed back up the alley and scattered, nearly knocking poor Tara over.

Tara followed the gunman. He was looking down the

narrow passages between the shabby houses of their alley, walking with firm steps. Most of the houses had their doors open. Thieves who came to this alley would know that, apart from the TV sets in some of the houses, there was nothing much to take. Even so, there was, now and then, a commotion in the alley when someone had their satellite dish stolen and spirited away from a broken-tiled roof.

The gunman took a large, crumpled piece of cloth from his pocket and held it to his nose. The smell of the kerosene, which Tara didn't even notice, was annoying him.

Tara watched as he passed down the alley. Her neighbour, Sundari, a young woman in her twenties with long, thick, black hair, sat on her doorstep. She was combing and oiling her tresses in parted sections, which she threw backward and forward with a flick of the neck, holding the others down with her hand. Tara wanted hair like that when she grew up.

'Oi, black face, did you see a yellow dog here?' the gunman asked Sundari.

'Not apart from you,' Sundari said.

The gunman passed on.

'If you're a hunter I can give you directions to the jungle. Get lost,' she shouted after him. Tara hesitated at her own door and Sundari turned towards her and then pointed her finger at Tara's open door. She was indicating that the dog had gone in there.

'In there?'

Sundari nodded and she slapped her thigh a few times, as though patting the flank of a horse.

Tara didn't know what she meant. Sundari was playing a game with her because, some months earlier, her grandfather had asked Sundari never to speak to Tara again. It was when Tara had started carrying oil for the shops. Sundari had accused Tara of spilling some oil on their stone doorstep as she passed that way, dragging an oil can with a great effort.

'Clumsy little bitch! Who'll clean that off?' Sundari had said. Grandad had heard her and come out into the alley. 'Don't ever talk to my granddaughter again. Just keep your filthy mouth shut. Or I'll shut it with my slipper.'

Sundari obeyed the order to the letter. She wouldn't say a word to Tara, even though Tara was desperate to talk to her. Sundari was the belle of the alley. She wore her saris tight round her hips, and that made Tara's grandad even more disapproving of her.

Tara went into their house. It consisted of two rooms. In the front room they slept. The back room was the kitchen. Their tap and toilet were in the common yard at the back, which they shared with six neighbours.

There was no sign of the dog in the front room. Tara hesitated. Then she heard him. He must be in the kitchen.

'*Kyaaoon, kyaaoon.*' It was a soft, whimpering cry.

Tara went into the kitchen. In the corner stood the masala stone, a flat and heavy five-sided slab flecked with little white indentations to make its surface rough. It was the stone on which Tara ground the spices for cooking. It was washed and on its side, leaning against the kitchen wall.

Tara saw that the yellow dog had got into the gap between the stone and the wall. He stopped whining when he sensed that there was someone else in the room. He was hiding.

'I won't shoot you,' Tara said, and she made the kissing

sound people make to call dogs. But she didn't want to get too close. The dog might bite her.

'Come on out,' she said. 'Shoo!'

The dog didn't move.

Tara got the broom that stood in the corner – a bouquet of brown rushes tied with rings of string near the handle. Using the soft end, with which she swept dust from the floor each day, Tara prodded the dog. She could see his behind shivering, but he didn't move. His tail was between his legs. He cowered behind the stone.

Tara pushed the broom harder and further. The dog tried to make himself small and disappear completely behind the stone. Tara put the broom down and, with an effort, tilted the grinding stone over till it crashed on the floor with a dull thud.

The dog clung to the wall, shivering. His refuge had been taken away. The eye that faced Tara was wide open in a terrified circle, and the black pupil darted about from Tara to the wall and back around the room. His ears seemed to be listening for the shot of the gun. Perhaps he thought the loud crack of the falling stone was the gun. Tara could see he was only a puppy – the fluff of his coat was only just turning to stiff hair on his neck and back. He was much smaller than she had thought when she saw him run in the street.

The dog tried to drag himself a few inches forward. Tara now saw that one of his hind legs had become a swollen bag of skin. It was shattered and limp, and it stuck to the body at an odd angle. The rickshaw had maimed the dog.

'Oh, no, you poor thing,' Tara said aloud. She fetched some water in one of their brass bowls. If her grandad saw that he would be furious. She put the water down in front of the dog and made kissing sounds to attract him to it.

The dog craned his neck forward and slowly approached the water. When he saw there was no danger, he fell upon the bowl and began licking it thirstily. Tara tried to touch his head to stroke it. He looked a mild, sweet dog. But the dog growled and pulled away, and Tara knew he was about to snap because he looked in pain and puzzled and bared his teeth.

Tara moved a few steps back. She got the feeling that she was being watched, so she swung round.

She was being watched, but it wasn't her grandfather. It was the gunman, standing in their kitchen with his rifle pointed to the floor.

'So, running in houses, eh? My most biter, my yellow cocker, my little darleeng,' said the gunman. 'Making your old uncle dance, is it?'

'You can't come in here,' Tara said. 'This is my grand-father's house. He'll be back now and he'll call the police.' The dog left the drinking bowl and cowered against the wall. He obviously sensed that the gunman was not a friend.

The man grinned.

A thought struck Tara. Maybe he *was* the police. She had heard that some of them were called 'plain clothes', and this fellow had very plain clothes.

'Get out,' she said.

'I am not come for any purpose, missy, but to shoot the dog and go,' the man said. By his accent and the droopy moustache, she could see that he was not from the town or from this part of India. He was a man of the south, who spoke in his own particular way.

'You can't shoot him in here,' Tara said.

'I tell you, missy, you open this door there and I'll kick him into backyard and "pop", I will get him there.'

'I won't open any door. You better get out,' Tara said.

'What's the matter with you, little girl?' the man said. 'Just once look at its teeth. It's going to bite you. It's most dangerous biter.'

'He's just a stray yellow puppy. He's showing his teeth because . . . because you chased him under the rickshaw and he's hurt his leg. Can't you see? And he's scared,' Tara said.

'Ah, you are not just a little girl, you are a yellow-dog specialist, are you? Well you'll die very painful, missy, with rabies. The yellow cocker will jump at your throat and tear out the flesh any minute and then what will you do? And your father? You will cuddle up and die.'

'Don't talk rubbish,' said Tara. 'The only thing wrong with this dog is that his leg is badly broken.'

'Now you've become doctor?'

'Doesn't matter what I've become, just get out of our house.'

'You see what you are doing wrong? You give the bastard some water in your bowl? Most catching thing rabies, more catching than mouse trap, more catching than tax inspector.' He laughed, but Tara didn't understand his joke.

The man walked to the back door. It was unlocked and its metal bolt and hinges were rusted through. He opened it. The dog watched his every move. The man then went through the front room and slammed the double front doors of their house, rattling the iron chain hanging from the top into which a padlock was threaded when the house had to be secured.

57

Then he approached the dog to kick him. The gunman's hat was still on his head and his gun was on his shoulder. The dog ran behind Tara for protection, cowering close to the back of her legs.

The man's grin broadened and he aimed a kick round her legs at the dog's mouth, like a footballer getting beyond an opposing player. The kick was well aimed. It caught the dog in the muzzle and he yelped. Still he didn't move.

At the same time Tara screamed, 'No, don't! You can't shoot here!'

'What is all this screaming for, missy? This a gone case dog,' the man said.

'This dog's done nothing to you,' Tara shouted.

The man smiled as though this was a novel thought. 'What can he do? Dogs don't do anything to me. They are not paid to do anything to me. I do things to them. I kill them.'

'Why?' Tara asked.

'Because man is man and dog is dog,' he said.

The dog was licking his lips with a dry tongue. He crouched as though trying to make himself small and invisible, even though he couldn't have been more exposed. The man could have shot the dog dead if he had wanted to.

'I don't want to scatter its brains all over your kitchen, missy, so please step one way. Then I'll be coaxing him into the yard, the son of a bitch. And quickly it's all over.'

'Why do you have to kill him?'

'Because I am the town Dog Shooter. That's my job, my work, since three years now. Stray dogs, on the streets, *dhishoom dhishoom* – dead.'

'He's not on the streets,' Tara said.

'What are you saying? Look at the rascal. Mud and shit

all stuck in him hair – that's what he is usually eating also. Look at his skin with all hairs fallen.'

Tara saw for the first time that the dog did have patches of mangy skin, but it didn't disgust her.

The man saw that Tara was distracted. He dodged past her and lunged with his slippered foot at the dog's broken leg.

Now the dog moved. He saw the open door and ran out at an even pace, limping. The man put his gun to his shoulder and turned the muzzle to take aim. The dog ran towards the little six-inch parapet that surrounded the communal tap in the yard. Tara hurtled past the Dog Shooter and threw herself on top of the yellow dog.

'Get out, missy, I am shooting,' the man said.

'You can kill me first, then you'll be hung for murder,' Tara said.

'What is all this?' the man said. 'This is not belonging to anyone, this dog.'

Tara's arms were now outstretched and she was kneeling on the ground in front of the yellow dog. The dog licked her elbow and gave her a start.

'It's my dog,' Tara said desperately. She didn't like to lie, but this was a matter of life and death.

'It's a free dog. A pariah. All ownership dogs are having collars,' the man said.

'This one can have a collar,' Tara said.

'I didn't see any collar,' the man said. 'Any dog with collar I am not shooting. Not allowed.'

'Then I'll get the collar,' Tara said. 'Can you wait one minute?'

'To check if dog is claimed? Yes, five minutes. That is the rules,' said the Dog Shooter.

Tara ran into the house. She took the belt she had bought for Grandad's trousers out of the plastic bag and approached the dog with it. The dog didn't growl at her now. The Dog Shooter looked on amused as Tara wrapped the belt of soft leather four times round the dog's neck and then, pulling the end out, buckled it. She looked at the man triumphantly. Now he would go away.

'That is not a dog collar. That is man's belt. Not sufficient. Sometimes peoples are tying up rabies dogs with belts and strings and ropes. That is not good enough. It's not counting.'

'What would be counting?'

'Only proper collar, going round one time.'

'Will you wait one minute before shooting him?' Tara asked.

The man was glum. He was holding his rifle despondently.

Tara went to her grandad's wooden shelves, and took his razor blade and the pair of scissors she used for her sewing. She ran back to the yellow dog, undid the belt and, measuring it for size, cut it with the blade to fit round the dog's tiny, bony neck just once. Then she started to pierce a hole through the leather so the buckle would fit it. She found she wasn't strong enough. The scissors wouldn't go through the leather. The Dog Shooter watched for half a minute as she struggled and the scissors slipped and cut her, drawing blood.

'Show it here, missy,' the man said. He slung his gun over his shoulder and took the belt and scissors from her hands. He pierced the leather easily.

'It has to be in the right place.' He made a second hole in

the shortened belt just in case, and handed it to Tara who collared the dog.

'That is a good collar,' the man said. 'But when your daddy come home he might kick out the pariah and then he will be a stray dog again and then I could shoot him.'

The man was right. He looked thoughtfully at the dog.

'You spoilt a good belt there, missy,' he said. 'Must have costed plenty money.'

Then he turned and left. Tara saw that the ends of his lips were bent downwards; but they didn't look cruel, they looked sad.

Tara thought of what he had said. Her grandad would come home and he wouldn't want anything to do with the yellow dog. She would have to put him in the street again and then the Dog Shooter would come and get him. The thought made her stomach flutter, and a rush of blood seemed to go up her neck and to her head, making her shudder.

The dog must be hungry, but she only had rice, which she had cooked when she came home that evening from the special holiday celebrations at her school. She put some of it in the same brass bowl, broke a raw egg over it and mixed it in. The dog ate it all and wiped the brass bowl clean with his tongue, making it move along the ground as he licked, chasing it and dragging his sagging limb all over the yard.

Suppose the dog did have rabies? Suppose he'd infected the brass bowl? Soon her grandad would be back. And now she had to face the fact that she had destroyed the belt which was to have been his Diwali present. What could she do?

Their neighbour, Sundari's mother, came into the yard from her kitchen door and went to the tap. Seeing the dog, she began screaming, 'Who brought this in here? Hey, Bhagwan! A wild beast. What will become of us?'

'He's only a wretched dog, not a mad tiger,' Tara said.

She lifted up the little fellow in her arms.

She would have to put him out in the street. But the dog collar would protect him, at least for a while.

She put the dog out and shut the front door. She would shut him out of her mind. She had to cook more food for her grandad.

Tara was glad she had made more rice when her grandad returned home and said he was hungry. It had been a hard day holding ladders. Diwali meant more lights, and more lights meant more bulbs to change and wires to fix – and the emergency crews still hadn't completed their rounds.

'My dear, I will have to leave you early morning. I am sleeping a bit and then going on extra work shift – Diwali morning shift, for which they are paying double because no one else has volunteered. And from today I won't be holding the ladder. Just for tomorrow I will get my first bulb-electrician job back. I will be changing the bulbs. Good money.'

Tara said they would find the money useful and that she was glad, but he must be careful climbing the ladders again. She said nothing about the dog. She was happy for Grandad. She was awake when she heard him get up, go to the yard to brush his teeth, dress, tinker with the lock of their single, small wall-cupboard, and then go out.

She was awake most of the night thinking about the yellow dog. He must have gone back to where he came from. Perhaps she was deluding herself. Perhaps he wasn't safe and she was just salving her conscience by persuading herself that he was protected by the collar she had put round his neck. There might be other dog shooters hired by the town. Would they see the collar and assume that the yellow dog belonged to someone? Or was a pariah clearly a pariah, which had to be shot?

She had no school the next day. It was Diwali. She was going to make her grandad some sweets out of lentil flour and sugar. She got down to her cooking, lighting the kerosene stove, and then, above its gentle roar, she heard the whining outside the door.

Tara hadn't admitted it to herself but she had been listening out for it. She went to the front door and pushed it open. Standing half on their single stone step, with his back legs collapsed beneath him, was the yellow dog. He was still wearing the collar. He looked up at Tara. She lifted him up. His broken leg, which hung off his body like a stone in sack, must have hurt when she tried to gather it up gently because he whined. But when he was shoulder-high he began to lick Tara's face. His tail was still tucked under him, touching his belly.

Tara took him through the house and into the backyard. Again she had to face the fact that she didn't know what dogs ate. But she'd give him what they had. She brought the chapattis from the previous night's meal and offered them to him. The dog swallowed them and his little belly bloated out.

The dog stank. Tara took him to the tap and, fetching some rags, rolled him over on his back and washed his matted, mud-clotted hair. The dog lay quietly, curious at this novel procedure, but not protesting at it.

What was she to do with him? Her grandfather would be furious if he even knew the dog had been there. He hated dogs. And she had destroyed the present she had bought

63

him with her last rupee. Now his trousers would never stay up on their own. Her plan of surprising her dear, dear grandad, who had looked after her all her life, had gone all wrong. She had never given him a real present before. As a child she had given him flowers and leaves she plucked from the municipal park, and stones she found in the secret places to which children go behind the houses and beside the streams. But now she had earned the money, saved it, and it was all gone with nothing to show for it but a collar round the neck of a yellow dog.

Someone rattled the chain on the door to the street, and without hesitation the Dog Shooter walked in. He wasn't wearing his hat and Tara could see that he was younger than she had thought, but that he was a young man going bald.

'Dog is dangerous. I spoke with Head Office. You have to give me it over,' he said. 'You can't keep wild dogs, missy, because it is too nefarious.'

'The Head Office is telling lies,' Tara said.

The man gave a contemptuous laugh. 'Does your father know this dog is alive and present?' he asked.

'It's my grandfather. And no, he doesn't know. Why do you want to kill the dog?'

Tara nearly said 'my dog'. She was beginning to think of it as belonging to her. But she stopped herself.

'Look, missy, I am knowing this dog don't have rabies. But I've got to live.'

Tara didn't understand. 'He is not shooting you,' she said.

The man laughed. He squatted on his haunches next to her and the dog. 'It's Diwali. I need cash,' he said. 'I have a daughter like you. Three. And I got no money for buying gifts.'

Tara still didn't understand.

The man put his hand out and the dog sniffed it and then licked it. The man turned his hand over to let the dog lick his palm as he talked.

'Every dog I am executing, I get money,' the Dog Shooter said.

Of course he did.

'So our friend here is finished. My job.'

'Can't you find another dog?' Tara pleaded.

'I can't,' the man said. 'I was chasing six dogs today, but the cunning buggers all ran into the temple where there are plenty people who don't like me coming with my gun. They shoo me off from there.'

'But you haven't got your gun,' Tara said.

'I've got it, but I didn't bring in here. I thought if your father . . . grandfather liked the dog, maybe he would do something for me if I would help him for keeping it.'

'He doesn't like dogs. He has been bitten too many times when holding ladders and changing street bulbs.' Again, Tara didn't understand what the man was getting at.

'When is he coming home? Surely it is holiday? You can tell him you love it, this dog, and he could help me.'

'Help you?'

'I am a poor man,' the Dog Shooter said.

At last, Tara knew what he meant.

'Just wait,' she said. She remembered that in the early hours of the morning, as he left for work, Grandad had carried out some transaction in the little wall-cupboard.

She found the key that he kept under the pillow. She went to the cupboard and opened its lock. In a small bundle on the shelf she found one-hundred-and-one rupees. Grandad's savings?

Tara knew she shouldn't take them, but the man was in the yard and she had to make him go. She felt a ticklish emptiness in her stomach as her hand grasped the notes and she counted them again. She was stealing, but she must stop thinking about it. Just do it.

She took the money and thrust it on the man.

'Now go,' she said. 'And promise you'll never shoot the dog.'

'This is not enough,' the man said. 'Not enough for presents for my wife and three girls.'

'Don't be so greedy,' Tara said. 'You'll never get one-hundred-and-one rupees for shooting one dog. So get out. But first, promise.'

The man counted the money again.

'Remember, little girl, I never come in by forcing and steal your money. We did business. You gave it of your own heart. I never even ask to you. So no tricks with the police or complaining to your grandfather or anything.'

'You have to promise first,' Tara said.

The man understood. He raised his hand in a mock oath.

'I promise not to kill this . . . this *peela*, this yellow dog.'

He had given the dog a name: *Peela*, which meant yellow.

The Dog Shooter left and Tara picked up Peela and kissed him. When would his leg heal? Would it always be crooked? There was no animal doctor to which Tara could take him, and even if there was it would cost money. If it was hurting, why wasn't he crying? Poor Peela the pariah. She put him down and he followed her into the house, dragging the broken leg behind him and giving out a yelp of pain as it bumped over the threshold.

'No, you can't come in here,' Tara said. Her grandfather mustn't find the dog here. He'd be there any minute and if he found Peela, and the door of his cupboard unlocked, and the money gone, he would be angry and hurt and confused. She was a thief. How could she explain the dog and the missing money and her treachery?

Tara's heart sank as she heard footsteps in the street. Too late. The footsteps stopped for a moment at their door.

The chain clanked. It wasn't her grandad. It must be the vegetable wallah.

'Wait,' Tara shouted.

The Dog Shooter came through their front room into the kitchen.

'I brought your money back, missy. Here.'

He thrust the notes at her.

'Don't you need it?' she asked.

'I do, but I am thinking a lot that I don't take money from little girls. It may be that my fate is that I execute dogs and swear many bad words, but I haven't become so low a dog myself to cheat money from small girls. Keep your money.'

Tara held the notes. She looked towards Peela. He suddenly looked like he had flat tyres.

Tara shouted, 'No, no, no. Not here, out.'

But it was too late. As Tara and the man watched, a yellow stream emerged from under Peela.

Tara ran for the rags she had left in the yard. She pushed the dog aside. She brought in the rusty bucket, filled it with water and, as the Dog Shooter watched, she cleared up the mess.

'My grandad. Oh God, my grandad,' she said.

'Clean up, I won't let grandfather in. I will threaten him

67

with gun. Dirty bastard dog. Must have training, not to do *soosoo* in house.'

'What about your girls? And Diwali?'

'I know what will make them all happy,' he said.

Tara could not guess what he meant. She stood up with the rag in her hand.

'A little yellow dog?' said the Dog Shooter.

He took Peela away. Tara put the money back and locked the cupboard. When her grandad returned he went to the cupboard, took the money and went out. She knew where he'd gone. He never missed buying her a Diwali present.

And this time he returned with her first sari.

'I tried to save some money for a gift for Diwali . . .' she began when he presented it to her and she unwrapped it from its white tissue wrapping and saw that it was green and gold and gorgeous.

'Hush,' said her grandfather. 'All I want is to see you in it. But I don't know how to tie a sari. I suppose you could ask Sundari next door to teach you – if she'll speak to you.'

Shyama Perera

Shyama Perera was born in Moscow where her father was a diplomat. In 1962 her family came to London and her father left – not to be seen again until she grew up.

'One Small Step', linking man's first walk on the moon with Mala's own jump into adolescence, is based around Shyama's life in Paddington with her determined and courageous mother.

At seventeen, Shyama got her first job as a trainee reporter. She later became a home-news journalist on the *Guardian* and now works freelance for tabloid and broadsheet newspapers. In 1982, she co-presented *Eastern Eye*, Britain's first English language programme for the Asian community, where her pink hair caused outrage! She still appears on TV and is also a regular radio broadcaster.

She lives in London with her two daughters, Nushy (Anyusha) and Tushy (Tushara), and writes novels. Mala is also the narrator of her first novel, *Haven't Stopped Dancing Yet*, which chronicles our heroine's growing-up years, from eight to twenty-one.

One Small Step

Shyama Perera

It's one of those dates that sticks in your memory forever: the twenty-first of July 1969. Thinking back, it was the week the summer holidays started, but the days that followed have left no imprint. What I remember about the twenty-first of July was that man walked on the moon.

I was almost twelve and my Auntie Rishi was throwing a party to celebrate her engagement to a toothy man with the darkest skin who'd come from Sri Lanka. In the photographs, he reminded me of a ghost from a story my mother had told me: Kalu Kumar – the black prince – a guardian angel who could only be seen in reflection, and who protected blessed souls in their sleep.

Ma had said I could wear my new dress: blue-and-brown check with a hooped zip that ran from belly button to neck. 'Groovy' we called it in those days: 'That's a seriously groovy dress, Mala.' It was very grown up, actually. Which was unusual because we were younger for longer then, if that makes sense. We believed in ghosts, like Kalu Kumar, and witches and fairies right up until the moment when secondary school robbed us of innocence and threw us into a world of new terminology: smocks, sox, wet-look boots, sex, drugs and rock 'n' roll.

That same day, my friend Janice's older sister, Allie, had come round after school and talked about free love. Someone had written FREE LOVE – just like that, in huge black capitals – on the white wall outside the estate agent's on the corner.

'Well, it's all the rage, innit, free love?' Allie said, adjusting a slingback stiletto. 'Be who you are, be who you want, with who *you* want. Let it all hang out. Hang free.'

Afterwards, my mum bristled in her nylon sari. 'I don't want that girl coming into this room again, Mala. These westerners. Chi! Free love? Don't they know that nothing in this world is free? That everything comes with a price?'

She slapped the roti dough harder and harder on to the Formica work surface in the little alcove that passed for a kitchen in the Paddington tenements. 'Janice should know better than to listen to that nonsense. You should know better! Hippy-chippy, what use is any of this if she can't even get five O levels?'

Part of me, the sensible part, agreed. But there was a new voice in my head that questioned everything Ma believed in. Allie wasn't a slapper by any stretch of the imagination. Peter Gill's sister had slept with half the red watch from Warwick Avenue fire station, and Kelly Grey's sister, Mary, was up the duff by a *black* man. The whole street was in a flap, including my mother who claimed she didn't dislike black men any more than she disliked all men, but nonetheless his colour was added to her catalogue of complaint.

'You see, this is how they end up, black and white. From the gutter they drag themselves further down, into the sewer. You say I'm old-fashioned, Mala, but we Asians have moral codes. We understand that nothing in life is easy, and we are prepared to work for it.'

'But my dad ran away, and he was Asian.'

My mother didn't answer as she rolled out the roti dough and cut rounds using a teacup. I knew that Allie was far too sensible to end up like Mary Grey, but Ma was convinced that girls bought the birth-control pill on street corners the way hippies bought hashish on Portobello Road on a sunny Saturday afternoon.

'If these girls buy the pill, they won't get pregnant will they, Ma?' I said.

'How do you know about these things?'

'So they're clever girls, not stupid?'

'Mala, I don't want to hear you say these things! Is this what Allie says? I wish you didn't mix with that family.'

Lovely Allie, such an enigma to my mother who, alone in a strange country, had developed a fear of the unknown. She saw so much she didn't like or understand and she didn't want to get any closer – to risk infection. But she'd got it wrong about Allie, who was fifteen, fearless and straight as a die. Sometimes Allie would let me and Janice hang around with her, and she taught us things.

'I enjoy the chase with guys, but I don't let them in for the kill,' she told us one afternoon, walking up to Paddington Station. 'Act mean and keep 'em keen. When I lose it, it'll be to someone special. You be the same when you grow up, all right? Silly to chuck it away on a fumble with some idiot behind a wall on North Wharf Road.'

Pulling on my new checked dress, I gave up arguing with my mum. She had fixed views on everything, from Harold Wilson to the price of the eels that were kept, alive, in giant white tubs outside the local MacFisheries. But I couldn't resist rubbing her up the wrong way one last time. After all, another ten weeks and I'd be twelve – the oldest girl in my new class, probably. I should be able to ask important questions.

'Ma, do you think Allie's the sort of girl who goes top-less at Woodstock?'

'Chi! All these western girls showing their breasts! They have no shame. No decorum. In our home country, Mala, a woman is a . . . woman.'

'But we're here, Ma, not home.'

'That doesn't mean you have to take on their terrible ways. It is possible for you to enjoy the best of both worlds.'

The best of both worlds! I wasn't even getting the best of *one* world. My entire life, it seemed to me, was a series of chores, interspersed with homework and warnings about situations I didn't even recognize, let alone experience.

My mother sniffed to herself as the rotis cooked. 'It starts in America; soon it will come here.'

'What?'

'Pop concerts. You hear my words. Peace and love.'

She said 'peace and love' like you'd say 'Jack the Ripper' or 'increased income tax'. But those words fuelled us. All of us kids greeted each other with a two-fingered salute: 'Peace and love, man.' Peace and love. It was beautiful!

Mum's voice receded to a background drone as I admired my dress in the mirror. I was filled with excite-ment. Rishi's getting married, and tonight Neil Armstrong will land Apollo 11 on the moon! How fantastic. How *bloody* fantastic.

*

It seems so far away now. Because nobody's walked on the moon since then. Not one footstep more in over thirty years. Sting sang a song about it: *Giant steps are what you take, walking on the moon.* Giant steps: they looked more like bounces really – like the Clangers' – when I watched the walk on TV the next day.

It's strange. They've sent probes to Mars and to Venus and there are space stations circling this planet every twenty-four hours. We operate satellites that can see into each and every room of any house in the world and eavesdrop on every single telephone call. But every time there's footage of man walking on the moon, it's the same footage that I would see for the first time that summer of '69.

That night, on the threshold of puberty, on the verge of upgrading from child to pre-teen, nothing could have been more exciting than the NASA space expedition. Perhaps, thinking about it now, it was because man was entering uncharted territory – just as my mother had done by bringing me to England. To the big rooming houses of Paddington where my father had put us up in a bedsit, sharing a bath and toilet with the occupants of thirteen other rooms, before disappearing into the ether, just like that. He'd left Ma alone and unsupported, to raise me. But that was *her* uncharted territory, and while she was a stranger in a strange land, trying to find a path forwards, I was a citizen of that strange land and everything looked utterly straight and simple to me.

Except that soon I too would embark on an unknown journey, swapping gobstoppers and Lucky Bags for spots, boys and hours of homework. For David Bowie, Roxy Music and Showaddywaddy.

*

Ma took the rotis off the two-ring Baby Belling electric stove that was fitted in identikit bedsits around the city. The little window was open and the milk she'd left on the sill to keep cold looked curdled. 'Eat now, or you'll be waiting till nine to be fed. Now Rishi has a man to run behind, we may not eat at all.'

'Is it an arranged marriage?'

'Nothing is arranged.'

'I mean, did their parents introduce them?'

'They're old enough to introduce themselves, Mala. The woman is nearly thirty, for goodness' sake. Why don't you concern yourself with more important matters?'

'Like what?'

She didn't answer, tightening her lips instead and popping the plate on my knees as I sat on the bed.

Everyone was at Rishi's: Anu, Seeli, Vimala, Shanthi, Oliver, Manel, Prisky, Palitha . . . There was a baila tape playing noisily, and Auntie Lata was doing an arm-flapping dance to its calypso rhythm and singing along: *Malu, malu, malu* – fish, fish, fish.

She was not the only entertainment. Everyone was watching Rishi's boyfriend, Arthur. In honesty, he wasn't quite as awful as he'd looked in the photographs that had been passed round at a recent reception at the Commonwealth Institute.

The teeth were still oversized, but a brilliant white, and now that the legs were also on view, the belly was more a pillow than a barrel. As Arthur's laugh boomed across the room, everyone was hooked.

Spotting my mother deep in conversation with Vimala, I

scooted over, but they immediately slipped into Sinhalese. Whatever they were saying, it had to be good!

'Not everything is appropriate for the ears of children, Mala,' Ma said when I challenged her.

'But I'm not *children*, I'm nearly twelve. I'm me.'

'Why don't you find a book to read?'

'What? The Bible?'

My mother coloured at this because Auntie Rishi was Christian, and I'd said the name of their holy book in the same disdainful voice my mother used in private.

'Please don't be rude. You're becoming a scallywag.'

'Then *you* don't be rude and talk in Sinhalese. It's no different to whispering.' I knew I'd overstepped the mark here, but she could hardly give me a slap with everyone around us. 'You're probably talking about sex again,' I added archly. 'Who cares if Rishi looked flushed when we called round here on Saturday?'

My mother had developed hot spots on her cheeks. 'Be quiet. What's got into you tonight, child? Do you want to upset every single person in this place?'

I looked at her mutinously. 'But I heard you say that.'

Now Vimala joined in. 'You and your mother live in one room, Mala. Sometimes you'll hear things you shouldn't. You must judge what is appropriate and what isn't.'

'Like telling Mrs Tilak about her nervous tic, you mean?'

'And what happened then? The poor woman didn't venture out for three months after that.'

'But we made plenty of vows for her, in the temple.'

'There may have been more deserving vows we could have made on behalf of our friends if you didn't open your mouth so easily,' Vimala scolded.

After I'd publicly referred to Mrs Tilak's physical shortcoming, she had barricaded herself indoors. My mother was mortified. 'I promise you, Mrs Tilak, it is not a problem. I merely mentioned to the child that when you are stressed, you get a little tic.'

'Where do I get the tic?'

This had thrown us all because we thought she knew.

It was only years later that I realized that each of us comes out a certain way, and to ourselves we're just fine. It's others who eat away at our self-esteem by pointing out flaws.

Anyway, Mrs Tilak had refused to come to any social events and in the end a whole posse of us had gone to the Buddhist temple in Chiswick to light joss sticks, chant and pray for her rehabilitation.

Going home with little orange prayer threads tied around our wrist, we passed that luck to Mrs Tilak in a bid to lure her out, and eventually our efforts had worked.

But now, I turned my back crossly on my mother and Vimala, not wanting a replay of past misdemeanours, and exited rapidly through the nearest door, to find myself in Rishi's backyard.

Around me the houses of Gloucester Terrace loomed disproportionately in relation to the small handkerchief of garden space. These days they'd probably call it a patio and charge some unknowing fool a million pounds for the privilege of putting their pots in it, but our part of West London was grotty in those days. A yard was a yard.

Most of the houses in the area were owned by a Sikh conglomerate. They rented them mainly to white people but there were some other Asians around – people like us, who'd pitched up from nowhere and felt like nothings. Well, my mother felt like nothing, anyway. She felt conspicuous in her sari and she said we smelt like 'curry puffs' because we lived in one room and the odour of cooking stuck to our clothes despite endless airing. London was cranking up for the bouts of racial violence that became known as 'Paki bashing' and Ma sensed the growing tension. The burden of responsibility made her old before her time. But it wasn't an anxiety I shared because England was all I'd known, really. I was part of it, not apart from it.

'You mustn't draw attention to yourself, Mala.'

'All I did was say good morning to the bus conductor.'

'One day the bus conductor will spit in your eye.'

'Why?'

'Because we're different and they don't like us.'

'Then let's make them like us.'

Once, when I was waiting for her outside a shop, a lady stopped and asked where I came from. I said Sri Lanka. She smiled and replied, 'Ah, Sri Lanka, such a lovely country. Why don't you go back there?'

I'd thought the woman was nice and chatty. Ma said she was a Powellite: a follower of the MP Enoch Powell who claimed having immigrants in Britain would lead to rivers 'foaming with much blood'. No wonder Ma was always scared.

'Walk faster, Mala.'

'I'm walking as fast as I can.'

'I can hear the gangs roaming in Leinster Terrace.'

Also, of course, there were the pros. Lots of raddled-looking prostitutes plied their business up by Paddington Station. They targeted Sussex Gardens, which was awash with short-term lets filled by migrating labourers. Hair-dye wasn't so well developed in the 1960s: 'loose' women were marked out by their canary-yellow and jet-black locks. One of them, Valerie, lived in our street. She'd give us kids tea on her afternoons off. Her legs were mottled with bulging veins and she seemed ancient.

'Are those support stockings, Valerie?'

'They are, Janice.'

'How did you get them veins?'

'We've all got them, dear, it's just that mine are varicose.'

They certainly looked very coarse, but I didn't ask if that was what she'd meant. Valerie was an unfathomable source of wonder to me. She had a notice in the newsagent's window offering French lessons but, as I told my outraged mother, there wasn't a single book on her shelves.

It was only much later that I learned that 'French lessons' was a euphemism for the services Valerie offered her male clients . . . No wonder she'd laughed when I asked about her pupils!

Sex, sex, sex: it was everywhere. It made my poor mother frantic. She adhered to the rigid moral codes of an ordered society, but had washed up in London just as the West was pulling the fabric of morality and decency apart.

She didn't see progress in the questions being asked; she saw confusion because the answers weren't clear. She didn't see intellectual curiosity in the way young people were experimenting with life and pushing at boundaries; what she saw was a lack of focus and an inability to conform. And conformity was her shield: our shield. It provided us with rules we understood. It was our security. Like Rishi getting married to a respectable man from a good family. We weren't just celebrating her happiness that night, but the enforcement of a workable order.

*

By ten, the party was warming up. The peach wine was flowing and even Ma was a little giggly. But I stayed in the yard, cheesed off at my exclusion from gossip and revelry.

Luckily, Arthur had taken the TV outside because it improved the reception from the small set-top aerial. I switched it on. *Ready Steady Go!* was the only programme I enjoyed – like *Top of the Pops* but cooler. Really. They had this serious babe called Cathy McGowan with brown hair to her waist and the shortest dresses and the whitest boots. She'd sit there giggling with the big stars like Adam Faith and Georgie Fame and Tom Jones. The Rolling Stones played live. But tonight it was just the usual serious stuff – God or politics or African rhino or something – and despite the TV being outside, there was still a snowstorm across the screen.

I banged the set – a completely acceptable cure at the time – and then kicked at the paving stones angrily because the picture started strobing instead. I was filled with a sudden anger – and I focused it on Ma because it felt like everything that went wrong in my life was her fault. I hate my *bloody* mother, I thought. Why does she treat me like some moron who doesn't understand what's going on?

As I stood seething, the ultimate horror happened: bossy Auntie Anu came out. 'How are you doing at school, Mala?'

'Fine.'

'Looking forward to a new start in September?'

'Sort of.'

'It's fantastic that you got into a grammar school. Don't waste it.'

'I haven't even *started*!'

'You must work very hard and reward your mother's efforts.'

'They were *my* efforts.'

'Don't be stupid – your mother has given up everything for you.'

'She hasn't given up nagging.'

'For goodness' sake grow up, Mala.'

'I'm *trying*!'

'A good education will pay your bills.'

'I don't have any bills.'

'Why are you so difficult, Mala? Always you sound as if you're speaking in exclamation marks. Is it too much to ask of you that you study hard and use your education instead of wasting it?'

Education: it was all I ever heard. Education was going to save me from an impoverished future cleaning toilets or selling nylon tights in Woolworth's. Big deal! It wasn't that I didn't believe it. It was just that the advice was taking on the rhythm of a mantra: school-learning-job-money-school-learning-job-money. Oh, yawn. If they didn't watch it, George Harrison would take the words to India on his next visit to the Maharishi Mahesh Yogi and turn it into a Beatles song . . . Crossly, I went back inside the flat.

'Ah, Mala! Long time, no see. Doing well at school, I hear.'

'Yes, Uncle Oliver.'

'And what will you study at university? Medicine, perhaps? Law?'

'I'm eleven years old.'

'Never too young to plan for the future.'

Crosser still, I went and sat in a corner, on one of the leather chairs bought at great expense from Frederick

Lawrence. With her leather furniture and new gold Humber car, Rishi was a good catch. She was a doctor who'd intended returning home after her studies, but, when the time came, enjoyed the freedom of London too much to give it up. Now she said she was happy to sign away that freedom to Arthur, a man from a good family who designed bridges. Dental bridges as it turned out, but I didn't know that till later. His overbite wasn't the finest clue.

My mother called me over. Reluctantly, I went.

'Why doesn't anybody ever say anything nice?'

'What are you talking about, child?' She picked a fish cutlet from the table and popped it into my open mouth. 'Rishi has made them with tuna instead of mackerel, but they're very nice.'

'I'm always being asked about school.'

'You should be happy that people show an interest.'

'Why can't they ask me about other things?'

'Because going to school, Mala, is what you *do*.'

Somewhere inside I knew talking to me about school was no different to grown-ups talking to each other about work, but I resented it. Because the endless lectures always allied study to me being different from the majority of kids: an immigrant. As an immigrant, apparently, education was extra-important because it was my only escape from poverty and discrimination, and the powerlessness they bestow.

'You've been blessed with brains, Mala,' Ma would say.

'But if I'm really that clever, why do you keep repeating everything as if I can't remember from the last time?'

'In this country, you are nothing. Just a coloured face with no status. You have to go out and earn it.'

'Everyone has to go out and earn it.'

'But it's harder for you.'

I hated that. It made me feel like I had a disability or a hideous disfigurement that made me less capable of achievement. It was like she too was finding things wrong with our brown skin instead of telling the racists to bugger off.

My skin was my badge of identity: a declaration of my history and my culture. An additional point in the game of success. I thought everything about me was terrific. (And I knew the red-headed boy from Carroll House thought so too because he always winked when I walked past.) But Ma was experiencing life on the periphery of British society, with people who considered her 'other'. I was growing up alongside those people, and if they were sometimes rude or ignorant I just put them right. I saw myself absolutely as their equal, their colleague – and, usually, their friend.

Taking a handful of the fish cutlets, which really were delicious, I mooched off to a quiet corner. Not that it was quiet for long. This time it was my Auntie Prisky who cornered me.

'Your mother says you don't want to talk about school, Mala.'

'No, I don't.'

'What would you like to talk about? Boys? Is there someone you have a crush on?'

'No!'

She laughed. 'Methinks the lady doth protest too much. What's happened to Nicholas Titchener – wasn't that his name?'

I blushed furiously. 'I never liked Nicholas Titchener!' It wasn't quite a lie. I never liked him – he was a show-off and he'd kissed Debbie Flint in the playground. But I *loved* him. And it was my business – alone.

'Then let's discuss your hobbies, Mala. Do you still keep that Stanley Gibbons stamp catalogue? Do you still spend your pocket money on facsimiles?'

'Stamps are babyish.'

'Nothing to replace stamps? Perhaps not. Is Janice still your best friend?'

'Yes.'

'And her sister. What's her name?'

'Allie.'

'Yes, Allie. I see her sometimes loafing around, flirting with boys outside the Stowe Club. She must be nearly fifteen.'

'She's already fifteen.'

'A very pretty girl. But don't grow up like her. Are you planning any summer adventures with Janice?'

'Yes, we're going shopping in Whiteleys.'

Prisky ignored the sarcasm. 'You know there's a big summer mural project at the library?'

'Boring.'

Prisky sighed. 'It seems to me, Mala, people talk to you about school because it's impossible to discuss anything else.'

I didn't like this. I got up and prowled the room. I heard Prisky tell my mother that she thought I was hormonal and there was lots of laughter. I knew it was about periods. We started later then: at thirteen or fourteen.

Eventually menstruation would catch me unawares and I'd almost have a heart attack when, going to have a pee, I'd find my knickers filled with blood. I would think I was bleeding to death. Right then, though, on that fateful night in 1969, it was just another humiliation that the adults in the room wanted to lay at my feet.

Around midnight, tired and bored, I wandered outside again and saw these magical words on the screen: *Man has landed on the moon.* I read them again and again. *Man has landed on the moon. Man has landed on the moon. MAN HAS LANDED ON THE MOON!*

For that millisecond, as the enormity of it sank in, and before I ran inside screeching with excitement, my heart stopped. The memory brings a lump to my throat even now. Because science was so fresh to me, and everything from the clothes we wore to the music we played to the cars we drove was about pushing ideas to their limits. Each new achievement moved me. I was wild with the joy of it! And the adults were too. They streamed out into the yard and we all just stared at the screen, filled with wonder.

The next morning Neil Armstrong took his first step and put himself on the map and human beings firmly in the greater universe with the immortal words: 'One small step for man, a giant step for mankind.' America had won the space race. The Russians had given us Yuri Gagarin, the first man in space. Now the Yanks had one-upped them in the most spectacular fashion. The achievement was as much about politics as science, but I didn't realize that then.

And for me, it had an importance beyond history. It is my first remembered stepping stone: a giant step for mankind, and a giant step for Mala too. I knew my whole life was about to change. That I was going to enter the adult world, albeit in a minor role, and that the things I did and the decisions I made in the years to come would colour my life forever. It brought me out in goosebumps.

86

Over the next few years, as I started to juggle all my different interests and priorities – exams and romance, music and make-up, clothes and hobbies – I was a little more circumspect about what I said to whom. I learned it was better to rehearse arguments than lose my flow and my advantage in the heat of the moment. My ma and I battled less, though I still had trouble giving in, even when I knew I was wrong.

I think everyone, everywhere, associated that night with a global coming-of-age. We moved from the realms of fantasy to reality: from chemistry sets in the front room to real science, real technology, real adventure. If we could walk on the moon then anything was possible. I believed it then, and I believe it now.

That night I even saw my mother filled with a fantastic optimism. 'If we can conquer planets, Mala, there is no excuse for ignoring the problems of earth, which are much easier to resolve.'

On the way home, she stopped at a chocolate machine and bought two bars of Galaxy. We sat on the stairs outside our room at one in the morning, savouring the taste.

The next day, Janice and I perched on the wall, straddling the words FREE LOVE, and talked about it all.

'It's funny, isn't it?' Jan said. 'It's not really anything to do with us, but it's exciting. Like when President Kennedy got shot.'

'That was awful. My mum cried.'

'So did mine. Because they're Irish Americans. Like us.'

'You're not American.'

'We're Irish. That's enough.'

She pulled on her liquorice bootlace. 'This is the first day of the rest of our lives. Six weeks' time, you and me will be in different schools, with different friends and different interests.'

'Don't say that. You'll always be my friend.'

'That's what Allie and her mates said to each other four years ago, but it wasn't true.' She sighed as tears welled in my eyes. 'Another year and Allie'll get a job. She'll end up with a baby and then what? Decades of the same. Just like my mum: four kids, family allowance on Monday and a chip-pan fire every Friday because she's watching Mike Yarwood. That's growing up.'

I was momentarily silenced by her profound observation. 'We don't have to go the same way. *You* don't have to go the same way. Stop sounding like Eeyore. My mum says girls in the West lose their innocence too quickly. Don't be so old.'

'That isn't what your mum means by innocence.'

'I don't care what *she* means! I know what I mean.'

'I hate being a kid,' Janice said.

'It's better than being a grown-up, though. Isn't it?'

'I don't know. Ask me again in ten years' time.'

'By then people will be living on the moon. We could emigrate.'

'And neither of us would be strange or stupid or different. Would your mum let you, Mala?'

'Not unless I'd got my A levels.'

We started to laugh. 'It's great that we've got men on the moon, isn't it?' Janice said.

I nodded. 'Yeah. It's the most important thing that ever happened.'

Aamer Hussein

Born in 1955 in Pakistan, Aamer Hussein grew up in his native city, Karachi. In 1968 he went to school in India, where he had often spent long holidays with his mother's family. He has lived in London since 1970. The London of his teens is the background of 'Tsuru'.

Aamer, who is bilingual in English and Urdu and also fluent in Italian, is interested in literature from all over the world, and divides his time between writing and teaching. He has published three collections of stories: *Mirror to the Sun* (1993), *This Other Salt* (1999) and *Turquoise* (2002). A volume of his selected stories, *Cactus Town*, recently appeared in Pakistan. His stories are frequently taught in schools and universities all over Europe and Asia.

Tsuru

Aamer Hussein

1

When they first became friends in early autumn, Tsuru disapproved of Murad's companions, Jime from the Côte d'Ivoire and Vida from Ghana. Tsuru wondered what an Asian could have in common with someone from Africa: was it merely dark skin? She didn't even pause to think about the differences between a Japanese and a Pakistani.

But after meeting Tsuru, Murad hardly had time for anyone or anything else, even his studies; in late November, before the end of term, Mrs Fogg-Martin had phoned his father to complain he'd missed two of her afternoon poetry classes.

As often as he could, Murad would go back with Tsuru to the flat she shared with an Australian girl called Pam and a Canadian boy named François. Sometimes they'd sit in the communal sitting room and listen to Tsuru's collection of American, English and Spanish records. But Tsuru thought that her flatmates were scroungers; she couldn't stand their marijuana joints and the cheap Rioja they loved drinking, and transferred her record player to her bedroom. Murad learned to smoke with Tsuru; or rather, he taught himself to smoke in his own room, choking, spluttering fumes out of his open window towards the empty patch of land people said was the burial ground of the Tyburn martyrs. Soon he was buying a packet of Player's every day – the cheapest he could find – and telling his father the price of sandwiches in the canteen had gone up.

The tutorial college they attended was in a shady residential street just off Gloucester Road. Tsuru lived a walking distance away, in Airlie Gardens; Murad lived off Marble Arch, and he soon discovered he could save fifteen pence a day by taking the bus, which cost less than the tube, from Park Lane to Cromwell Road. In the afternoon he'd get off just past Hyde Park Corner and walk home through the park; that was even cheaper, and it helped him save for the cigarettes he bought to replace those he'd accepted from Tsuru and her friends.

When he'd arrived in London in May with his sister to join their father, the park had been, along with the library and Selfridges, their main field of entertainment. There were regular rock concerts – Mungo Jerry, the Kinks, and once the hallowed Rolling Stones. Mahalia Jackson sang gospel unaccompanied, and her voice hung over the park like a rainbow. There was also the spectacle of hippies smoking hash and making love in the grass, and Hare Krishna people who handed out lentils and rice to passers-by. In those days they'd had no friends; and films, which they'd seen all the time in Karachi, were expensive unless you sat in the front row near the screen. They went to see Bombay movies once or twice a month at first, possessed by a nostalgia that was almost entirely imaginary, since they'd always had a preference for western films at home. Passing through the dingy suburbs that seemed to make up most of London filled them with genuine pangs of homesickness for the leafy lanes and elaborate gardens of the neighbourhood they'd left behind in Karachi, or made them miss the broad, airy avenues of the district they'd lived in for three years in Rome. Then his sister had gone to her fashionable girls' boarding school in Norfolk and he, to save time, had been sent to Elliott House to rush through the O levels he'd already prepared for in Pakistan.

Most of the boys in Murad's school were Greeks, Arabs and Iranians, and older than he was; they drank, gabbled away loudly in their own languages, and chased after girls in pubs. Many of his schoolmates didn't wash enough because they thought it girlish to shower more than twice a week, or their landladies simply wouldn't allow them to. Each group seemed to identify with a national or regional label, playing roles written for them by some invisible scriptwriter. There were Malaysian Chinese boys and girls who banded together; Hong Kong Chinese who only had time for their books; and East African Asians who patronized Pakistanis because they considered them backward and insufficiently westernized. So he made friends with the Africans who had fluent English and open minds.

In the evenings, he would stop by at the local library on South Audley Street. Then, unless his father was taking him out to dinner with acquaintances who had offspring with whom he was expected to become friends, he'd usually stay at home with a book, or very often watch exotic films with titles like *Ashes and Diamonds* or *Yang Kuifei* on late-night television. He was developing an interest in Japan through the films he'd seen and a handful of novels he'd found in translation at the library – he was particularly taken with one called *The Sailor Who Fell from Grace with the Sea*.

When Tsuru came back to school from holiday he was struck by her elegance, which reminded him of the ivory beauties he'd read about, though she didn't strike him as beautiful at first because she seemed so fragile. She usually dressed in black and her hair was ear-length. She had a nearly perfect oval face; her skin was like smoked cream, her eyes were long, narrow and fringed with blade-sharp lashes, her full mouth parted to display very white and slightly protruding teeth. She sat down at the desk next to his, but they hardly spoke until one afternoon when, without knowing why he was doing what he did, he followed her out of the school building after the literature class, to the row of shops on Marloes Road. She was going to buy cigarettes. He lingered under a low tree till she emerged from the tobacconist's, then fell into step with her for a block before asking her if she'd like a cup of coffee at the nearby Wimpy Bar on High Street Kensington. She smiled, unsurprised, and said yes. They talked a little, mostly about classes. Then Tsuru told him she was nearly eighteen, and had lived alone in London since her father, a JAL employee, had been posted back to Tokyo two years ago. Murad, who'd turned fifteen the spring before, told her how his mother had stayed back in Karachi and planned to join them in London the next year. When they finished exchanging life histories it was nearly five-thirty. Murad reached into his pocket for money to settle the bill and found he only had five pence, and it would cost him half of that to get to Hyde Park Corner. He couldn't even pay for his own coffee, let alone Tsuru's. But almost as if she hadn't noticed, Tsuru said, 'You can buy me one next time,' and put twelve pence on the quarter plate. That was her way: she'd pay for him quite thoughtlessly once, and another time let him treat her, or even ask for a loan.

Later, she told him his blush had given away his discomfort: his blush was one of the many things about him that made him the butt of her jokes and teasing. 'Remember,' she loved reminding him in company, 'the first time you ever took me out for coffee you wanted to know if I was a virgin, and then you didn't have money to pay for our coffees? I knew you'd be a bad date right away then.' Murad couldn't remember whether this was true, or one of the many funny stories Tsuru liked to tell about him in front of others. He knew he had asked her about her love life, but thought they'd known each other at least a month by then. What he remembered was the way she'd repeated the word 'virgin', pronouncing it 'baaar-jin', though her English was usually unaccented. And he also remembered her answer: she'd 'played around' with a cousin when she was twelve, and then had had two boyfriends, one who was much older, and the one she was still seeing, Rick, who lived with his parents in Sevenoaks, where she often spent weekends. He was bemused, too, by the thought that she'd assumed he wanted to ask her out on a date.

Murad himself had come very close to losing his virginity with a childhood friend during a wedding celebration in Karachi, at which about ten teenagers had turned a late-night revel into a slumber party. But he and his putative sweetheart hadn't really known how to go

95

beyond deep kisses and long embraces; then, as they were fumbling with buttons and bindings, they'd been inter-rupted by people getting up for drinks of water and visits to the loo. In the morning they were still technically virgins. By the time he'd been in London a few months, he thought it best to be honest, at least to Tsuru, about his inexperi-ence. Anyway, he'd never met anyone remotely suitable. You had at least to like someone a lot to make love with them – and he, where would he meet that someone who'd like a person as awkward and plain as he felt he was?

Tsuru thought his innocence was quite funny and announced it to Pam and François in his presence as soon as she could. 'The little darling, shouldn't be a problem with his looks, he's a nice-looking bloke,' Pam hooted. Murad felt his ears and cheeks heat up.

'He's OK if you like dark types,' Tsuru mused, as if Murad weren't there. 'Me, I like blondes.' The word came out as 'bronders', Murad noticed, wondering why Tsuru's accent sometimes betrayed her. But he was aware then, for the first time, that it mattered to him what Tsuru thought about him, and that she shouldn't, as a friend, have made fun of him like that in front of Pam.

2

'What does your name mean?'

'Desire, or hope, I think. And yours?'

'A long story, that. A poor peasant saved a crane from a trap. Then a beautiful woman turned up at his door and said, "I'm your wife." She wove the finest fabrics for him, which he sold at a profit. She made him swear he'd never open the door of the room she wove in while she was working. One day he did, though, and he saw a naked crane weaving cloth with feathers plucked from her breast. She flew away then, and never came back. Oh, I forgot to mention: the wife's name was Tsuru.'

3

Last summer, the summer after the spring he arrived in London, had been bright and fresh, and he'd had to rush out to buy T-shirts and cotton trousers because the clothes his mother had had made for him to take to London were warm, tweedy and quite conservative.

Leaves fell in autumn and he hardly noticed the trees' stripped branches because he spent most afternoons with Tsuru, listening to James Taylor, Carole King, Cat Stevens and Melanie in her room. Just as he hadn't noticed that his hair, once short, then trendily layered, now fell to his shoulders, because his father hadn't been nagging him to visit the barber.

Then winter brought a blanket of snow for Christmas and Murad was lonely, lonely. His sister had come home for a day or two when the holidays began, and then gone off to spend the best part of the festive season at a farmhouse her new best friend Helena's family owned, deep in Dorset. Tsuru was staying in Sevenoaks over Christmas with her boyfriend, and Murad hadn't made any new friends. But on Boxing Day François and Pam rang the bell. His surprise was faintly tinged with pleasure – he hadn't even known they knew where he lived. They were going to the park – would he come with them? In Hyde Park the Serpentine was glassy. They pelted each other with snowballs beneath the evergreens and rubbed snow on each other's faces. He had never been in snow before, never even seen snow before coming here to London.

He'd always assumed, without really thinking about it, that Pam and François were together, but the way they teased each other about crushes, and the feelings of isolation they seemed to share and complain about, threw him in doubt. He promised he'd ring them in a day or so, but, in spite of his loneliness, didn't – after all, what, apart from Tsuru, did they have in common with him?

He'd done his O levels by then, and started studying for his As. Because school was closed till the second week of January, he'd taken to going to study at Kensington Central Library, which had a large reading room upstairs. Much of the time, though, he read novels – James Baldwin, Muriel Spark, Mary Renault and Yukio Mishima were his present favourites. But the true reason for his trips was that Airlie Gardens was just nearby and he hoped he'd bump into Tsuru, who'd never answered any of the telephone messages he'd left with François.

When he ran into François in the reading room for the second time in a week, the Canadian boy asked him back to the Airlie Gardens flat for a drink. He said yes only because it was Tsuru's place, though he knew by now Tsuru hadn't come back after Christmas: 'Not even to pick up her things,' Pam whined. 'She still owes two months' rent, and she's locked her room, the cow.'

The sitting room was large, dun-carpeted and on the first floor. A dim bulb disguised its grubbiness. There was a fire burning, 'You've Got a Friend' played on the turntable, and Murad was surprised by the ease he felt with these people who, a month or two ago, he wouldn't even have considered his friends. And the warmth seeping through him, particularly after he sipped the first glass of red wine he'd ever tasted, owed nothing to the thought of Tsuru. In fact, he realized, Tsuru had a way of making everyone revolve around her tastes, her wishes, her peeves. She'd made him see these friendly, lonely foreigners through her eyes, because something had made her turn away from them . . .

He looked at them: slight blond François dressed in denim jeans and matching jacket even in winter, smoking one of his perennial soggy joints, and Pam with her thick green jumper sliding off one plump creamy shoulder to reveal the upper curve of a breast. He'd always thought she was big – if not actually fat – before, but tonight, without the striking contrast of Tsuru's slight presence, the sturdy body and lush curves seemed quite attractive. They looked like a lady and her suitor in some old Dutch painting, he thought: the lighting and fire are just right, though the clothes are all wrong.

'And she kept trying to turn François against me, because she can't stand having any boy paying attention to another girl,' Pam was saying, her eyes as narrow and green as a cat's beneath her frizzy red fringe. Murad had been daydreaming and didn't know what had led to yet another Tsuru story, but Tsuru was what he, François and Pam had in common. And people did like to talk about her. He'd noticed that even at school classmates would pass remarks about her as soon as she left the room. 'You know, she walked into the bathroom one night in her bra and panties while François was showering; she'd had a fight with Rick. She just stood there and looked at him. François told her to get out—'

'Shut up, Pam,' François began, but a half-instant too late.

Murad had already said, 'I don't think we ought to be bad-mouthing Tsuru when she isn't here. At least she says what she thinks in front of us all.'

'Well, she said you were morose and childish and she spent time with you because you were so lonely – always following her around.'

Murad knew his face, already flushed in the artificial heat of the fire, was turning an even deeper red, that familiar blush again, and he was filled with mixed reactions: the pounding sensation in his forehead he identified as anger; the melting wax in his entrails was guilt. Here I am, he mused, sitting in this room I know only through Tsuru, listening to her music on her turntable, and enjoying her absence. But I don't believe she'd say such things about me.

He stood up to leave, but a conciliatory François was brandishing the wine bottle with one hand and tugging at his arm with the other, pulling him down to the cushion he'd been sitting on. Soon Pam was pouring even more wine into his tumbler and the semblance of cheer was about to return. At least they've got each other, he thought, they seem to do everything in harmony and be such good friends. And once again that lonely feeling he was so familiar with since Tsuru and he had said their abrupt telephone goodbyes before Christmas invaded him. Pam's tales had made him, if only for a moment, doubt Tsuru, the only real friend he'd made since he arrived in London.

On Saturday evening, he was back in the Airlie Gardens flat, surrounded by people dancing, lounging, smoking, accompanied by the strains, passionate but also plangent, of a Santana album. He couldn't imagine how Pam and François had crowded about sixty people into their sitting room, and wondered who they all were: they both complained they hadn't many friends. He was dancing slow, cheek against Pam's warm cheek. He, François and Pam had gone to an afternoon show the day before, and when Pam had excused herself to go to the 'little girls' room', François had whispered, 'She really likes you, you know,' and when she came to sit next to him he moved slightly closer. But before he could work out what to do next, she had his hand in hers and was licking and biting the knuckles of his fingers. Suddenly his fingers had found themselves in her blouse and her hand was reaching up his denimed thigh. The feeling that had started as a curious little furry animal when he had looked at Pam lounging by the fire the other evening was turning into something slyer and more predatory, a wolf cub gnawing at his lower belly. So now he knew why he was here. He'd told his father he was going to spend the night at François's, without mentioning Pam.

Pam was about five foot nine, and François probably five-eight, but Murad was over five-eleven, very nearly six foot. Pam could rest her head on his shoulder as they danced.

Murad awoke at five. Pam was snoring quietly beside him. He didn't have a key and he knew he shouldn't ring the doorbell before eight; his father would wonder why he'd left François's place so early on Sunday. He had a bad taste in his mouth after the half-bottle of cheap red he'd swilled again without liking it, and no memory of pleasure at all – only the feeling that if this grappling and wrestling was what everyone wanted to learn about, well, then, he'd learned it all quite easily and it was no big deal, just a slightly messy and uncomfortable collision of muscle and bone. And the heaviness of someone's body against his, sweating even in the chill January weather, had made him shrink to the edge of the bed at the risk of losing his part of the coarse red blanket. All last night's attraction had completely gone in the grey dawn light that seeped through the half-curtained window.

He rose from the bed, showered and washed till his winter-sallowed skin was red, dressed quietly in the bathroom and went into the sitting room where one figure, wrapped in a blanket, lay on the sofa. He thought of going into the kitchen to make some coffee. He knew where everything was, he'd often brewed drinks for himself and Tsuru to take to her room. But then he thought better of disturbing the sleeper. He hovered for a moment – he didn't want to go back to Pam's bed, because he felt guilty again about what he'd done, sleeping with a girl he wasn't remotely in love with.

Then he heard François's unmistakable Quebecois tones: 'What's up, man? Up so early? Can't sleep?' François lurched naked out of bed, draped his thin cream blanket around himself like a toga, and stumbled into the kitchen. 'Coffee.' It was more a statement than a question. He came out with two steaming mugs, handing Murad one stamped with the welcoming motto of some seaside town and embellished with a handle that was the head and torso of a hideous woman with protruding breasts.

'How did it go? Did you make it?' he asked, and the thought came to Murad: François does share her room. Her bed. I knew and didn't want to know. She threw him out so I could stay over with her. Suddenly he felt better, because if he'd used Pam she'd used him too. And then he felt worse: no, it was a game Pam and François had played, it didn't matter to them really, in some odd way they were using him to get back at Tsuru.

'She really fancies you, you know,' François muttered, reaching for some Rizla paper and a lump of the dope he loved smoking. For a moment, Murad wondered whether he meant Pam or Tsuru. And Murad saw that François, for all his streetwise ways, was probably no older than he was, maybe even younger, and he didn't understand the games Pam was playing, though he thought he did. And under the world-weary mask he was hurting.

Pam telephoned three times over the next two days. He spoke to her the third time because she called at eight-forty-five, and her persistence was wearing out his father's nerves. Murad arranged to meet her in the park at ten, and walked with her to a bench near the Serpentine. He'd splurged on a pack of Dunhills for the occasion. Lighting two, he handed Pam one, struck a brooding attitude, and said, 'You're a sweet, lovely girl, Pam. But it isn't going to work, you know. We're just light years apart.' He'd heard Richard Burton say something like that to Elizabeth Taylor on a beach in a film he'd watched on television late one night.

'It's that bitch Tsuru, isn't it? It was her you wanted all the time. You made a fool of me. Pig. You were thinking of her when you were with me. She slept with François, you know, even while she was with Rick. That's what she's like, she'll take on anyone if she's in the mood. Bloody scrubber. I'm surprised you haven't tried.'

Murad knew his mouth was hanging open and, for the first time since he was seven, his eyes were about to water.

'And you know what else? I bet her a bottle of wine to a Santana album that I'd have you in bed before she did. She said you'd never look at me. Ha, ha, ha, I say. And ha, ha, ha again.'

'I don't believe you,' Murad said. 'You're lying. You're muck.' He turned on the balls of his feet. Hoping she couldn't see how he was trembling with the effort to control anger and tears, he strode off through the park without saying goodbye or looking back.

4

Missing Tsuru was now such a habit, he'd almost stopped noticing how much he still did miss her. She'd become an image of everything he didn't have – companionship, affection, adventure. He hadn't tried to contact François even though he felt sorry for him, since there was no neutral ground for them to meet on. But François seemed to have disappeared along with Pam anyway.

Murad had signed up for English, French and History this year. A-level classes were held in a bigger building – further away from home, in Brook Green, which meant a longer journey there and back. Though his bus route took him past it every day, and past the Wimpy where he'd first sat with Tsuru and got to know her, he avoided using the Kensington library, because he just didn't want to see François: it would probably embarrass both of them too much.

He had new acquaintances, a handful of Pakistanis, Indians and Malaysians with whom he had coffee and cigarettes at school and, occasionally, met outside. He even had a new best friend. Shigeo wasn't in any of his classes, but they seemed to have the same lunch break on Tuesday and to leave classes at the same time on Thursdays, so when one day they found themselves walking towards the bus stop together and then getting on the seventy-three bus, they started talking. Shigeo was dark-skinned for a Japanese; he had a nimbus of coarse wavy hair, and a birthmark on one cheek.

'I'm getting off here,' he said, as the bus passed the Albert monument and approached Exhibition Road. 'Would you like to visit?'

Murad just smiled and followed him off the bus.

Shigeo brought up Tsuru almost immediately. She'd lived with her father in the same block as Shigeo before he went back to Japan.

'Miss Shimomura's very strange for a Japanese girl,' Shigeo said over a cup of tea in his narrow bedroom. He was squatting on the floor while Murad sat on his bed. Then, probably in response to Murad's quizzical expression, he added, 'Goes her own way. She's free. She borrows things. Money. She goes out with too many boys. She's noisy.'

How many boys add up to too many may be a matter of perspective, but one boy in all the time I've known her, if you discount Pam's lie about François, is hardly many from any angle – and she's hardly noisy, Murad thought. Then he recollected how once, after she left a room, he'd felt that she did, in fact, take over in a group, even in her silences, projecting a restlessness by sighing or running fingers through her soft hair. She also had a way of stringing together her sentences with gasps, sighs, digressions and subordinate clauses, so that even a simple story became a bravura performance. She could be an excellent listener, though, when there weren't too many others around.

'I didn't know you knew her that well,' he said aloud.

'Not so well . . . she asked me to keep some of her records for her when she was moving out of the building. She left behind a lot of strange records,' Shigeo told him. 'She still hasn't picked up some of them, but I hardly ever listen to them, don't understand the music she likes: wailing and screeching.'

As if to illustrate his point, he took the Janis Joplin album *Pearl* from a rack and, in an almost defiant gesture, slung it on the turntable. The bourbon-scented notes of 'Take a little piece of my heart' filled the room, but Shigeo kept talking, about music now. His passion was western instrumental music, and he'd studied violin since he was five or six, but had been discouraged by a teacher from training to become a classical musician. He'd switched to the guitar.

Though Murad knew nothing about western classical music, he felt compelled to ask Shigeo to play something. Shigeo's countenance darkened as he swooped and swayed over his Spanish guitar, his fingers rapid on the strings. He played two pieces, one of which had a vaguely Moorish feel. Shigeo stopped, wiped the perspiration off his forehead with a towel, and announced, 'I'm going to play something different now.'

The melody he played was simple, five notes repeated in different combinations, now playful, now melancholy. From time to time he'd pluck at a string with two fingers. Murad was put in mind of water falling on leaves, and then of wind whispering to water, and then again, there were echoes of some strange bird's song.

It couldn't have lasted more than five or six minutes, but Murad had closed his eyes and opened them after what seemed like an age. He tried to find something appropriate to say, but only came up with: 'What's it called? Was it Japanese?'

'I made it up,' Shigeo said. 'As I played. Right now. Shall we call it . . . "Cranes Flying"?'

As Murad was leaving, Shigeo picked up a bag, slipped the Janis Joplin album into it, and handed it to him with an incoherent murmur of explanation. He wondered if the reference to cranes had been deliberate, but he didn't know whether the Japanese word for crane was Tsuru, or whether Tsuru was just a crane in a fairy tale.

Somehow, people often seemed to assume he had access to Tsuru, or was the guardian of her things.

Sometimes he wondered: was it a growing need for companionship that made him respond to Shigeo's extended hand of friendship? His only real friend until now had been Tsuru and, when she left, Pam and François, who were her friends. Or at least he'd thought they were her friends until they'd proved to be no friends at all; instead of filling in the space she left, they'd only made it blanker. Perhaps the initial response to Shigeo had been because he was, like Tsuru, Japanese. But Murad couldn't think of two personalities so unalike. They didn't even seem to belong to the same world.

With Shigeo, the only effort Murad had to make was to go along with his invitations, which were, much of the time, issued as statements. 'Today we'll see *The Music Lovers* at the Kensington Odeon, it's about Tchaikovsky.' 'Today we'll try Indian curry.' 'Very sunny weekend, we'll go to Windsor.' Soon after they met, Shigeo's parents invited Murad out to dinner with his father, at a Japanese restaurant where they sat around a low table, as if they were kneeling, but actually there was room for them to dangle their legs in the well beneath the table. Murad's father responded by calling them to the house, where he fed ten people food he'd ordered from a fancy restaurant and had a protégé he'd hired for the evening, a student of accountancy who needed extra cash, serve it. There wasn't likely to be a great friendship, but, in good Asian fashion, once the parents had eaten together the sons were at liberty to see a lot of each other and even to stay out late on special occasions.

Shigeo bought a car on his eighteenth birthday, and he was willing to buy tickets, make plans, organize, and never seemed short of enough money to pay for two. When once, in passing, Murad mentioned his father had finally promised to take him, at his insistence, to see a production of *Hedda Gabler* with Maggie Smith in the title role, Shigeo sighed and said he'd been wanting to go to that too. Murad's father fell out of the plan as soon as he heard that someone else was willing to replace him. Shigeo was to use his ticket instead. After the harrowing performance, to get rid of the gloom that seemed to have overcome them, Murad suggested eating at a pizzeria adored by trendy students – a place he could afford on his pocket money. Shigeo, back in control now after having admitted his wish to do something Murad had wanted to do, said he couldn't stomach cheese and insisted on treating Murad at an expensive burger place instead. A renowned rock singer was dining with his entourage at the table next to theirs.

What Murad had once taken as oriental formality – you could hardly, after all, call Shigeo reserved – turned out to be a combination of self-possession and extreme moodiness. Shigeo seemed to know what he wanted from the world and how to go about finding it. He moved around London as if he'd lived there forever, though he'd only been there a little longer than Murad. At times, Murad wondered what the older boy, so serious and seemingly independent, saw in him; Murad was not a flatterer, and neither of the boys were demonstrative. Shigeo made it quite clear that he didn't want to have anything to do with Murad's school acquaintances. He'd move away politely if he found Murad in a group, or call off abruptly if he rang and Murad mentioned friends were over. Murad made sure to do exactly that – warn him there were people visiting – after Pinky, a girl in his history class, dropped in unannounced once while Shigeo was over at his house, and Shigeo was convinced the visit was prearranged. Shigeo didn't seem to have any friends of his own; when Murad shyly asked him about this, he said, 'Japanese teenagers in London are childish and boring.' Murad felt he'd been intrusive; Shigeo rarely asked personal questions, and it was often hard to remember what they talked about when they parted.

Shigeo could suddenly lapse into very long silences, which often didn't matter while they were at the movies or even immersed in their own thoughts as they walked in the park. Over cups of coffee, though, or sitting in each other's rooms, these silent spells would fall over them. And then Murad would think of Tsuru.

When the time came for Shigeo to perform a guitar solo, particularly if it was one of those wildly romantic Spanish melodies he favoured or something minor-keyed that seemed to have a Japanese feel, the music would somehow evoke Tsuru, her presences and absences, how she talked and talked about everything like a bird flitting from wire to wire, about travelling and poverty and family wars, and how he had something to say in response, always, even when he felt she'd lived so much more intensely than he had – this daughter of divorced parents, a free mover in a world he'd barely started learning to recognize . . .

And then he'd be encouraged to dredge out his own secrets, hurts and fractures and fears half-understood, so that even if he couldn't completely express himself or Tsuru responded as if he'd said something disingenuous or naive, he'd be left with feelings to examine and deepen. He'd started writing poetry then, and continued. Much of it came from rather dark dreams he had, or was inspired by music, or by those vague feelings of isolation from the group he sensed Shigeo shared with him. Once, in his room, he'd showed some verses to Shigeo, who'd hemmed, nodded his head, and said, 'Very good English, very good . . . mmm . . . images, but maybe a liiiittle bit above my head.' He raised both slender hands like a cradle above his bushy hair. Murad hadn't made the effort again, though Shigeo often asked him 'How's the poetry?' as if he were enquiring about an eccentric and slightly unsavoury relative.

One afternoon, when a conversation about something entirely trivial – the relative merits of western and eastern music, perhaps, or Ken Russell's style as a film director – was edging quite close to a display of tempers, Murad made an excuse to leave Shigeo, and, walking through the park with a spring drizzle descending, thought the time had come for them to spend time apart. Murad didn't like asserting his views and tastes the way Shigeo did. (Recently, when trouble had begun between the east and west wings of Pakistan, Shigeo had asked him about the situation as if he wanted to pick a fight, and Murad uncharacteristically retaliated by bringing up Japan's treatment of Korea. But that was a long time ago, Shigeo said. Japan had learned its lesson.) What, after all, did they really have in common, apart from their loneliness? Being foreign boys in London? Their dark hair and eyes? It wasn't as if Murad was planning to drop Shigeo: he'd just avoid him for a while. Their friendship had become too much like a habit.

He didn't answer the phone that weekend. But there weren't any calls except one from Pinky, his Pakistani classmate, who wanted to borrow some history notes. She came over on Sunday; they strolled down the Bayswater Road to look at ethnic bric-a-brac and some terrible amateur art. He stayed home on Tuesday because he had a headache and a very sore throat. But when the doorbell rang at eight and Shigeo stood in the doorway with a heavy Mates bag in his hand, saying he'd been late-night shopping and had dropped in to see why Murad hadn't been in for his Eng. Lit. class, he had to admit he was relieved. Shigeo didn't accept a half-hearted invitation to stay for supper; he left after an hour, a cup of coffee and a cigarette. It was only after he'd gone that it occurred to Murad: the shops on Oxford Street stay open late on Thursday evenings, not Tuesdays.

5

On Saturday, Tsuru called him from a phone booth on Bayswater Road: 'Meet me in the park!' He slipped a pair of soft moccasins on his bare feet and went to meet her by the Peter Pan statue. Tsuru stood silhouetted against a backdrop of spray from the fountains. Her hair was longer, shoulder-length, cut raggedly at the edges; she'd gained a little weight. Her long eyes were edged, unfashionably, with black kohl, and even in May she was dressed in a black polo neck and a long black skirt. She held out her arms and he went to her, bending down to kiss her proffered cheek. 'You've grown taller,' she whispered. 'I feel like a midget.'

They walked across the park to the cafe on the bridge, to which they'd often come before.

'Where did you go, Tsuru? Where've you been? Not a message, not a postcard . . .'

'I went home,' she said. 'To my mother, this time. She sent me a ticket. I'm back at Rick's, but we don't really get on any more, not the way we used to . . . You know, he just isn't growing up and I treat him like a little brother and that drives him really mad, and his parents just don't relish the tension or even understand what's up between us, so I'm looking for a room in Kensington, to be close to the school again; I'm coming back in autumn. Have you taken Spanish? I want to take up Spanish again, and do French, too.'

Time passed without his noticing. Every question elicited a detailed answer from both of them. He realized how much he'd been talking; he hadn't talked so much since she left, and he was suddenly embarrassed by the sound of his own voice. He started laughing when she said, 'Hey, calm down, we have time.' Then, leaning over the stone slab that served as a table, he put a hand on her hand and kissed her cheek, nearly spilling her coffee. She blushed and grinned. 'Calm down, shaggy dog. I'm glad I'm back, too.'

That's the way it is with Tsuru, he thought. She knows what I'm feeling without my having to say anything. But he didn't want to talk about François. Or Pam. And she hadn't asked.

112

Then he remembered. He looked at his watch: five-fifty-five.

'God, I'm supposed to be at Marble Arch. I'm supposed to meet a friend at the Odeon.'

'Oh, I was counting on spending a little more time with you. Well, I can catch the six-twenty-five from Victoria, I suppose. Walk me?'

'I'm late already. The show starts at six.'

'Stupid of me to think you'd be free to drop everything, even for your old friend who hasn't seen you for a long, long time, on a Saturday evening. Who are you seeing? Anyone I know? Girlfriend, by any chance?'

'Boy, actually. No, you don't know him . . . well, yes, you do a little. Shigeo Matsubara.'

'Matsubara? That creep with the Spanish guitar? A friend of yours? His father works for JAL, too; I suppose you know he lives in the block we used to be in. Well, he's such a girl, you might as well have chosen a girl instead. You've moved fast while I was away, I must say. Following my tracks, were you? François, Shigeo, and Pam . . .'

'Who told you about Pam? That's all a mistake, anyway.'

'That you kept phoning her after I left? Stayed over on New Year's Eve? And went back to Airlie Gardens three times and pestered her until she'd had enough of you and told François to throw you out?'

François, throw me out? he thought. He's more your size than mine.

Lies, lies, he wanted to say. Instead, he blurted out the story about Pam and what she'd said, the backbiting, the bets.

'I? Bet Pam you'd sleep with her? Me? Would I care?

113

Well, yes, I would care, I wouldn't expose any friend of mine to such trash.' (She said 'tulash' in her excitement.)

He'd made her miss her train now, she said; but he could go off to see Matsubara, she'd just wait alone at Victoria Station for the next.

He thought it best to continue with his arrangement. To give her the upper hand now would start him, once again, on that road he'd been on before, of waiting for her calls, bearing her absences, putting up with her snide remarks and sarcasms. 'Look, Tsuru, I'm sorry, I didn't start anything, but if you want me to I'll say I'm sorry, I'm so glad you're back . . .'

Tsuru was laughing soundlessly, as she often used to do when he started stumbling over his own words. 'Listen, I almost forgot. Open this. Put it on.' She took out a little box in which nestled an exquisitely crafted watch with a silver strap. 'For your sixteenth birthday. See? Even in Japan I was thinking of you on the day.'

For the second time that day, he leaned over to kiss her cheek. But it was her mouth that met his, warm, moist, slightly open.

6

It was past ten by the time he got off the bus at the Speakers' Corner stop, after seeing Tsuru on to the nine-twenty-five from Victoria. Never having been in a situation like this before with Shigeo or anyone else, he didn't know what he should do. Phone and apologize? Shigeo's father would pick up as he often did in the evenings, and Shigeo would probably refuse to take his call. But when he came to his block he saw Shigeo's car parked in the drive. Shigeo must have seen the film on his own, come out and called, and Dad must have told him I wasn't back yet, Murad thought. Now I'll be in trouble because Dad won't know where I've been, and he'll think I'm lost or that I've been lying about seeing Shigeo.

Shigeo had rolled down the window of his car and, cigarette in hand, was beckoning to him with that palm-downward gesture of extended hand which had disconcerted him when he'd first encountered it – in Pakistan it would be considered rude, but it was usual among East Asians. Murad went over, apologies making his lips feel like jelly, but Shigeo merely gestured him into the car.

Murad didn't ask where they were going. Driving through the park towards the Albert Hall, Shigeo told him he'd waited at the cinema till the film began, missed the first few minutes, then phoned from a coin-box when he came out to see where Murad had got to. No one had picked up the phone. He'd phoned again several times. So it was fine, then; Murad didn't have to worry about Dad wondering where he was – Dad was out, and if he came back and didn't find Murad at home he'd assume he was with Shigeo.

'A friend called me,' he said. He thought Shigeo deserved some explanation. 'I thought I'd have a cup of coffee with her in the park and come along to meet you at the Odeon; it wasn't that far away, I could have walked there in a quarter of an hour. Then we got talking, I hadn't seen her in months. It was Tsuru. You probably guessed, anyhow.'

(There was more, so much more, he wanted to say. We walked, hand in hand, to the round pond. The sun hadn't set but we could see a pale, full moon. We sat and we talked and we talked, but I couldn't tell you what we talked about. I wanted to tell her what I felt about her, what I've probably felt about her since we met, but I couldn't. I started to say something, but she put her finger to my lips. I kissed her hand and then I kissed her cheek and then I kissed her mouth. I could feel her eyelashes, brushing my cheek. We got up and we walked to a tree and we lay down under the tree and I held her very, very close. She had her head on my chest and I could smell her hair. It was drizzling now and though I wasn't cold I was trembling and to my surprise she was trembling too. I felt as if nobody had ever touched me before. As if I'd never touched anyone before. I could say much more but I won't. I'll write a poem about it all. About her.)

Shigeo placed a restraining hand on his forearm.

'Let's eat. I'm hungry. Have you eaten yet?'

(Then she looked at my watch and she said: It's late. I have to go. I didn't say anything. I followed her. I took her to the station. She gave me her cheek to kiss as she got on to the train like she always does.)

7

At the All Night Burger place on High Street Ken, Shigeo ordered a lager with his food and drank it quite fast. Murad, who'd sworn off alcohol after the New Year party at Pam's, had ordered a Coke because he thought it looked childish to have a milkshake – which was what he really wanted – while Shigeo drank beer. Shigeo toyed with the chips on his plate, left most of his burger, and ordered another lager.

They sat silently over their plates for a while. Murad, who was famished, finished everything on his. Then he asked, 'How was the film?'

'Good. I'll see it again with you. Or maybe you can see it with Tsuru.'

Murad noticed that Shigeo hadn't referred to her, the way he usually did, as Miss Shimomura. He didn't reply. Murad could cope with Shigeo's silences, so maybe he should just have sat there silently and not mentioned the film. But this time he thought, Now I've started this conversation let's get it over with soon, then we can both go home and perhaps I'll write a poem. But Shigeo was still talking.

'Male friends are the only ones you can count on, you know? But as for you, you're in love. It won't last, though. Don't worry. I've been there. I know what it's like. Sorry, maybe I'm talking too much, but I'm drinking, and in Japan we say sometimes you drink just so that you can tell the truth about things. And you're my friend, so I think I should talk to you truthfully.

'I've been where you are now. I've had a girlfriend too. For nearly six months. First we were friends, then we became . . . We had so much we shared, background, tastes, language, and we were both foreigners here. We spent all our time together. We became . . . close, you know? I'd never been with a girl before in that way. But she had. With one boy, she said, but I began to think there were others.

'But she began to change as soon as we'd been together two or three times. Just because we were together in that way, she said, it didn't mean there was anything special between us. She wasn't in love with me. She'd loved her other boyfriend more. I'd get jealous and angry and I wouldn't call her for a day or two and then she'd call and we'd meet and she'd say I was her best friend and that's what she really wanted, a true friend, that's what was really important, and friends could make love too if that's what they both wanted, but if one of them becomes possessive then that's when the problems begin and making love makes everything so much harder . . . and I was trying too hard to hold on to her. She couldn't breathe when I did that.

'Earlier she'd felt that I was like the brother she'd never had, a younger brother, though we were about the same age. What she'd liked about me when we met was that I was gentle, soft and gentle like a girl, she said, but now I was acting like all the rest. Like her ex-boyfriend. Like her father, who'd chased her mother away . . .

'I got ill. I don't know what happened, but I was ill for many, many days. She'd come over almost every afternoon after school, sit with me, tell me funny stories about our classmates and Japanese kids we both knew. She'd hold my hand, sing, talk, and I thought we were really together.

'I got better. She didn't ring me. She didn't answer my calls when I rang. Then one day I saw her on the street and she told me she'd moved. She was sharing a flat with some friends in Kensington. They were having a party on Saturday. I would come, wouldn't I? And bring some beer or wine.

'I got there late, because my parents had some visitors. I walked into a dark room. Crowded and smoky. I couldn't make out too much at first, but then – I saw her. She was sitting on a cushion on the window seat with a boy. A blond boy. I recognized him. Her ex-boyfriend. They seemed to be arguing. But they were drinking from the same glass and taking drags of the same cigarette.

'I stayed where I was and if she'd seen me she didn't show any sign of it. Her flatmate came up to ask me if I wanted a drink and I said yes, followed her to the table where the wine was, filled a plastic glass and moved away. When I got back to where I'd been, they'd gone. I felt there was no point in staying on. My head was spinning, I felt suffocated there, it was summer and really, really hot. I don't know how long I stayed, a half hour? I remember the songs that were playing just before I left the party, 'Lola' by the Kinks and that song about the summertime that was so popular last year. I went on to the street. There was a car parked just outside the door. A two-seater. A couple in it, embracing very tightly. A blond boy and a girl with black hair. They sensed someone standing there and parted. The boy looked down, but the girl looked me straight in the eye.

'It was Tsuru.'

8

... *Somewhere, there's a country where cranes come down and change their form. In a land where there are cherry trees in the shadows of mountains with peaks of snow that never melts. And if you're lucky you'll save a crane from a trap and she'll come to your door and stay with you and spin you fine brocades. But you must never ask her where she comes from. And you must never open the door of that room in which she spins her secrets.*

That's what Shigeo did. He opened the door. And Tsuru flew away from him. I don't think he's lying about anything. I don't think he ever even meant to tell me about it, and even last night he was trying to keep her name from me, but it just slipped out. It can't have been another Tsuru, can it? No. I think the reason he was drawn to me in the first place is that he knew I was close to her. It must have been only a little while after they broke up that she and I became friends. Or perhaps she was still seeing him. But he said it was summer. Summer, when I got to know her, was nearly over . . .

Murad stopped writing. He had been trying to study that morning and then, when he couldn't concentrate, he'd made an effort to write those poems about his evening in the park with Tsuru: he'd had them in his head, word-perfect, with some semblance of rhyme. But what he'd written instead were these rambling passages about Shigeo and the story he'd told.

He'd come home very late last night to find the door locked from the inside. He hadn't dared to ring the bell and wake his father, but he wanted to pee and eventually he had to ring. Gingerly. But his father didn't answer. So he'd had to go down and ring from the call-box across the road – probably where Shigeo had tried to call from earlier. Dad had an extension on his bedside table and answered after about four rings. He'd let Murad in and said, 'Enough. No more late nights. I thought you'd had an accident. Your friend called and said he'd waited for you at the cinema and you hadn't showed up, and then he called again after the film, from across the road, and when I said you weren't yet back he said he'd thought you might have come in late and sat somewhere else so he'd looked for you but still hadn't found you. I want you home at eleven at weekends, and during the week you're to be back before eight. And you're not going out tomorrow or seeing Shigeo for a week.'

That was fine. He thought they'd need to be apart from each other for a while to adjust to the new circumstances. Because Shigeo, in spite of his warnings, must know that Murad was going to keep right on seeing Tsuru. And keeping Shigeo and Tsuru in different compartments of his life was going to cost a lot, because, whatever either of them said, Murad didn't want to be forced to choose between them. Unless one of them asked him to. He hoped they never would, because he knew who his choice would have to be.

And there was still so much he wanted to ask Tsuru. He'd wanted to call her: the impulse to lead her to the door of the room where she spun her secrets was overpowering. The door Shigeo had thrown open only revealed more secrets.

Tsuru had said she'd come back, next Saturday. He didn't think she'd have found a new place in London, so if Dad had cooled down by then he might just ask if Tsuru could use the guest room that night. Or for a few nights. Just having her close, breathing and sleeping so near . . . and she might, if he didn't press her or persuade her, tell him the whole story. Many stories.

For now, though, he had his own version of her story to write. But he didn't know if it was his or Shigeo's. Whether the hero, the boy the crane girl favours, was him or Shigeo.

It didn't matter.

He turned to a fresh page and wrote:

They say there was once a young man who fell in love with a girl called Tsuru . . .

As he wrote, he heard the wings of birds circling above his head, the sound of running water, and, in the distance, the notes of a guitar, echoed by the call of a flute and the soughing of the wind.

Bali Rai

Bali Rai has been writing seriously for several years. His first novel, *(Un)Arranged Marriage*, was published in 2001 and has now won three awards. He is also the author of *Dream On* (2002), *The Crew* (2003), *What's Your Problem?* (2003) and *Rani and Sukh* (2004). Having spent his time working as a bar manager whilst writing his first novel, he is now trying to cut it as a full-time writer, working on different projects and visiting schools to talk to his readers.

If he had to get a 'proper' job he thinks he'd probably opt for journalism. He has also dreamed of becoming – in no particular order – a footballer, a reggae superstar and a Bollywood legend. For now, thankfully, he is happy with being able to write what he likes for a living. Well, almost!

'Beaten' is his first published short story.

Beaten

Bali Rai

'*A* re you happy to submit this as it is?' asked Dr Khan.

Ranjit sat and watched the psychiatrist for a while before shrugging his shoulders.

'Dunno,' he replied, looking out of the window in Dr Khan's office.

'Let me read it back to you, Ranjit. OK?'

'Whatever.'

'Remember, this is what we will forward for your assessment.'

'I know,' replied Ranjit. 'Just read it . . .'

I suppose I should start by telling you a little about my old man and what he used to be like. He was a big strong man, a Punjabi who wore the turban and beard of a Sikh, but never understood that being a Sikh meant more than looking a certain way. His hair was black, but he was balding under his headgear. His beard held flecks of grey and red, and his eyes were the same honey-brown colour as mine – only his were ringed with the yellow of an alcoholic. He wore a saffron-yellow turban and dressed in tracksuits most of the time, his pot belly preventing the zip on his top from doing up. On each hand he wore big gold rings and around his neck a chain of solid Indian gold. He always smelt of curry and body odour mixed with a taint of booze, often faintly disguised by cheap aftershave. I can still remember how he smelt.

He was a taxi driver when he could get work, which wasn't often. He spent much of his spare time at the local Sikh temple, the gurdwara, where he sat on the committee that ran the place. Every couple of years there would be a new vote for committee members and every time my dad would be voted back in by friends and relatives who only saw his calm, confident, friendly face. They never knew the real man. Underneath the mask. It made him proud to be so well liked by his own community, and he'd talk about it constantly, to anyone that would listen. He saw himself as an important man. A big player. Boasting was part of his nature.

He was also a liar, a cheat and a hypocrite. Beneath the turban and the beard lay a violent man – a man who would beat his wife senseless in front of his children, under the influence of alcohol, whenever he'd had a bad day or lost a couple of fares. Sikhism forbids alcohol, but my dad hid his habits well – from the gurdwara, at least. He thought that he was entitled to call himself a Sikh just because he was a Punjabi. But the two things are so different, and he was never clever enough to see that. Like others I have met, he confused the two until they merged into one – in *his* head, anyway. He loved to drink Bacardi, Famous Grouse whisky and a home-made brew called *dhesi*, a drink popular in the Punjab. Almost every other night our house would play host to his loud and drunken friends.

He followed a pattern, my dad. He would wake in a foul mood, sweating and smelly. Once he had eaten his breakfast he would drive to the cab stand. Waiting around for jobs made him restless and angry. Stolen sips from his flask of booze meant that he could cope, I suppose. He'd finish work and head for the gurdwara, probably pissed already, then on to the pub, before somehow managing to drive himself home to demand his roti and dhal. At the weekend he'd eat lamb and curried goat and tandoori chicken, forgetting the vegetarianism of true Sikhs, which none of my family actually are. And on Sunday mornings he would rise with a hangover, his breath rancid with the smell of dead animal flesh and alcoholic spirits. He'd affix his turban and his pious nature, and then head for the temple, dragging me and my younger brother and sister in tow. Our mother would follow a few feet behind us, caked in foundation to hide her bruises.

He'd beat my mum almost daily. He'd beat her if his dinner was too hot or cold. He'd beat her if there weren't enough chillies in his dhal. If she dared to question his demands, he would kick her and punch her and drag her by her hair, pulling out clumps of it, in front of us kids. And if we tried to stop him, cried or screamed or ran away to hide in our rooms, he would say, 'Look at how you have made my children hate me, you bitch', and then beat her some more.

My brother, my sister and me learned from an early age to keep quiet. Not because we didn't want to help our mother and not because we didn't care about her. I can't sleep free from nightmares, even now, and my brother and sister, Balbinder and Harpal, have mental scars, which will never heal properly. We stopped crying out simply because he would have used our tears as a reason to lash out again. I remember beginning to think that it was our fault that he beat her so much. I would tell the kids not to make too much noise. To stay in their rooms. All for fear of awakening the raging beast that hid behind my father's beard. It made no difference.

I remember that he once bought me a bike for Christmas – a rusting frame with one wheel missing and no gears. He picked it up from a friend's garage. My mum simply asked him, with a smile, where the other wheel was.

He went crazy, punching her in the face and kicking her somewhere that no man should kick a woman, especially not the mother of his children. That was the day that I turned from being a scared child into an angry adolescent. I stepped between him and my mother for the first time, and caught two open-handed slaps that were meant for her. Hoping that he'd be satisfied by his assault on me, I moved away. But he was still raging and, as I left my mum unguarded, he struck out with a fist, smashing her nose.

She didn't even cry. She just stood there, holding her hands to her face as the blood poured from her nose, her eyes wide with shock and fear and anger. I blamed myself for it, reasoning that if I hadn't provoked him by stepping in, then maybe he would have just left her alone. I know now that there was nothing that I could have done to make him stop. Nothing legal, anyway.

He stormed off to the pub after that, leaving me with my mum. I begged her to let me take her to the hospital. To report him to the police and the social services. I even told her that I would tell them that he was abusing me and the kids – just to get rid of him – but she said no, just like she always did. She told me that she would be fine and that Punjabis didn't let their family business become public knowledge – it was dealt with at home. Not like all those idiots that you see on chat shows. It was her burden, she told me, that she would have to bear alone, regardless of the concern of my Aunt Sukhjit and her husband, Harinder, who had guessed what was going on. She told me to stay out of it, to let him do as he pleased. That she would rather have her kids safe and herself bruised than the other way round. That she wouldn't let the family name bear a loss of honour, of *izzat*.

I cleaned her up as much as I could before helping her to her room, desperately trying to shut out the questions and tears of my brother and sister. I cried myself that night as I searched for a way to make everything all right. But I was only thirteen back then and not as big as my dad. I couldn't stop him and I couldn't fight him. So I spent my time day-dreaming about how I would grow to be as big as him. I thought up elaborate ways to hurt him and to kill him and hide his body. I picked up tips from stupid thrillers and serial-killer novels.

Another incident that will always stick in my mind happened on my fourteenth birthday. My mum had arranged a party for me, inviting members of both sides of the family. My dad didn't like my mum's sisters – she has two – and on the day of the party he was in a real mood. His taxi was off the road because of a problem with the brakes and he sat at home all day, muttering under his breath and drinking cans of cheap lager.

The party was due to start in the evening, and my mum was busy in the kitchen, preparing samosas and curries and meat for the guests. Balbinder and Harpal were excited, racing around all day long, in and out of the kitchen, whilst I was doing my best to help Mum. Because she was so busy, she forgot to put salt into the chickpea curry. My dad walked into the kitchen around five that afternoon to try the food. He went straight for the chickpeas, putting some into a little steel bowl and picking a freshly fried samosa to have with them. The first mouthful he took must have been samosa alone because he didn't say anything. It was the second mouthful that offended him. He spat it out, throwing the bowl to the floor.

'What is this?' he demanded in Punjabi, scaring Harpal who had been playing near to where he stood.

Harpal started to whimper and looked at me, tears welling in her eyes. I gathered her up quickly and carried her to the living room. I left her on the sofa with a kiss, before returning to the kitchen.

When I walked in my mum was silent, hoping, I think, that my dad would just go after he had shouted a bit more. But he stayed where he was.

'Are you listening to me, you bitch?'

My mum looked at me and then looked down. 'Please, not in front of Ranjit,' she said.

'Not in front of *Ranjit*? Are you stupid? You think you are going to serve this muck to my family? To my *brothers*?' He was getting angrier and angrier.

'I'll change it,' replied my mum, shaking as she picked up the pot of chickpeas.

He grabbed the pot from her and took it over to the sink, pouring its contents into the basin.

'Change it?' he shouted. 'You'll make a new one!'

'Yes, I will,' said my mum in a whisper.

My dad turned to her and slapped her. As she stumbled, I tensed, edging forward.

'Come on then, you little bastard!' he said to me, then turned to my mum and called her a whore.

Tears began to roll down my cheeks as I stood still, helpless. Unable to do anything. Useless. A knife caught my eye. A big, sharp cook's knife, with a shiny blade. In my head I picked it up and plunged it into him, deep into his chest, driving down with both my hands. Blood spurted from the wound that I had inflicted as he crumpled to the floor . . .

SLAP! The image in my head vanished and in its place was my mum, on her knees, crying, my dad standing over her. I fought with the urge to jump at him and waited instead until he had finished shouting at my mum.

'God curse the day that I was married to this bitch from a family of whores!' he muttered, heading for the living room.

I helped my mum to clean up before the party started, and chopped the onions she would need to make a fresh chickpea curry. We were quiet and tearful. The party itself is something I can't remember. Or maybe it is just that I don't want to remember. Birthdays have never really bothered me too much since that day.

I hate going to school now, too. I mean I was never really that keen in the first place. The only things that I liked were English, history and football. But since my mum was put away I've lost interest in those too. See, the other kids – they aren't supposed to know about what happened. I moved to a nearby city and started at a new school, along with Balbinder and Harpal. But the city we came to, Leicester, has a huge Punjabi community and people like to gossip. The Punjabi kids at my new school know what happened – they've heard all about it from their parents. For a week or two my mum was plastered all over every newspaper and our story appeared on the local news as well. So now I'm the son of a murderer.

The other kids call me names and slag off my mum, and I've been in a lot of trouble. I get into fights all the time, and every week I'm sent to counselling sessions: one for the violence that rages inside me like some virus that I can't shift and another for me to talk about the years of violence I suffered at home – all the abuse that I witnessed. Well, that's how they put it anyway, the doctors. I'm not a big fan of counselling – it makes me feel like there's something wrong with me and I know that there isn't. Yeah, I could be less angry. Less violent towards the other kids. But they should stop calling my mum names and slagging her off. She's not a murderer. She's not a killer. She had to do what she did . . .

Yeah, I am happy with where we live now – with Auntie Sukhjit and her husband. They don't have any kids of their own and love having us around. My uncle, Harinder, is a million miles away from what my dad was like. He's sound. He takes me shopping and plays football for the local Sikh temple side. I get to go with him to the practice sessions and matches, which is wicked. It's a different game to the one that I'm used to watching on the telly. Players with any skill get fouled all the time and the air is full of shouts of 'Tek him out, innit!' It's not the beautiful game that Beckham and Owen play. It's more like war, with each team trying to hospitalize the other with elbows and bad tackles.

I've been watching loads of telly, too. Mainly the sport and the music programmes. I've also got into daytime soaps, like *Neighbours*. You know, the ones where everyone plays happy families all the time and the biggest threat is next-door's dog pissing on your lawn. The greatest dilemma is about what to take to the church raffle. The mums don't get beaten to a pulp by the dads whilst the kids cower behind sofas and hide in cupboards. Happy families. That's a different game from the one I'm used to.

You're the third child psychologist that I've been to – and I don't think that you'll be the last. I can't explain what has happened with remorse – I can only tell you what actually happened on the night that my dad died. The facts. I've told the police and the social workers, but for some reason they need me to tell you, too, because you're the expert, apparently. I just want you to understand that none of it involved Balbinder and Harpal. I don't want them involved. They're just kids. They weren't even there. They had gone to my aunt's – a little break for my mum. Man, they loved going to Auntie Sukhjit's. She spoils them rotten.

Harpal and Bal asked me why I wasn't going with them. Harps wanted me to read her a bedtime story. I told her I had too much homework and a science test to revise for – I needed the peace and quiet. But Bal told me that he was happy I wasn't going with them.

'This way,' he'd said, '*I'll* be Uncle Harinder's favourite and he'll take *me* to the footie – so there!'

He's spoken very few words since. He's got this problem communicating his feelings and only talks to me, Harpal and my aunt. He doesn't even speak to Uncle Harinder and he used to *idolize* him. I guess he doesn't trust older men. He's been to see various counsellors and doctors, but none of it helps. The only person who seems to help him is my aunt, whom he clings to like a baby. And he wets the bed, too. But then who can blame him. Not many nine-year-olds have seen what he's seen.

I'm getting away from the point of the story again. It's like I've got some unconscious need to hide the truth, I suppose. I bet that's what you'd call it. Anyway, Bal and Harpal left with my aunt, and I helped my mum in the kitchen. The old man had been hanging around all day, getting drunk and moaning because he'd been sent home. Again. He was in a really nasty mood, swearing and cursing my mum. We were having paneer, an Indian cheese, which she'd fried in a curry masala. She'd also made some tandoori chicken pieces, which I was tasting when my dad walked into the kitchen, hammered. I think it was around nine-thirty.

'Where's the Coke?' he demanded in Punjabi, holding a fresh bottle of Famous Grouse in his hand, and swaying with the effort.

My mum told him that there was a cold bottle in the fridge. He grunted, opened the fridge door and removed the bottle. I could hear a couple of his friends talking in the living room. They were loud and obviously as blitzed as he was. Every other phrase contained a swear word and I felt embarrassed having to listen to them in front of my mum. Embarrassed and angry. My dad looked me up and down and then turned back to my mum.

'Are you trying to turn my son into a woman?' he sneered, taking offence at my presence in the kitchen.

'No.' My mum didn't even look at him.

'I'm just helping Mum out,' I said.

'Boys do not help in kitchens,' he told her, ignoring me.

'But, Dad, I'm just . . .' I could feel the anger rising within me.

'SHUT UP!' he shouted, making my mum start. 'Or do you want me to beat some manhood into you?'

I glared at him, but he still wouldn't look directly at me. Why, I don't know. Maybe he was ashamed of being such a bastard. Maybe he was embarrassed. I didn't care. I was fuming.

'You could try,' I mumbled under my breath.

The fist came out of nowhere and caught me on the temple. The pain shot through my head, making my eyes water, but I stood my ground.

'You see what you teach your children?' he said to my mum accusingly.

'He didn't mean anything by it,' whispered my mum, moving to stand between us.

'Didn't mean anything! The bastard spoke back to me!'

He raised a fist, swaying on his feet, but didn't throw it. Instead he gave a sick smile – one that told me *he* had all the power. Dared me to do something about it. The big man, showing off his strength by beating people who were half his size. I didn't react, knowing that he would hit my mum if I did. Seeing that his little battle was won, he smiled again.

'Make sure that there is enough food for my friends and don't embarrass me tonight . . .' he warned.

I stood and looked at him as my mum returned to the cooker.

'. . . If you want to see the morning,' he finished, before heading back to his friends in the living room.

*

My mum and me had our supper just after ten, I think – it's hard to remember exact times. We ate in the kitchen, at a breakfast bar that I had put up with the help of Uncle Harinder. From the living room I could hear the sound of laughter and raised voices. His friends were eating and drinking like pigs at a trough. Each piece of roti stuck in my throat as I began to wonder whether his friends knew what he did to my mum. Whether they cared. Whether they, too, went home to beaten wives or beaten children. It was like trying to swallow golf balls, eating, as I considered whether my dad's friends turned a blind eye to his abuse of my mother. In the end I threw most of my dinner in the bin. My mum cleared our dishes and then told me to go to my room.

'I'll make them roti,' she said in Punjabi, 'now that they've finished the chicken.'

'I'll stay and help,' I replied, not wanting to leave her alone downstairs with my dad and his friends.

'No! Not with the mood he is in,' she said, ushering me out of the kitchen.

I protested for a while longer, but my mum begged me to leave her in the kitchen alone, telling me that he would only get angry if I stayed there. I relented and then walked through the living room, making a tactical error as I went. My old man told me to say hello to his friends, but I ignored them. At the time I didn't realize how much of a mistake that was. I didn't see the rage on his face. The anger in his eyes. And in a way, I'm quite glad that I didn't: it was his anger that made things come to a head.

I went up to my bedroom and sat on my bed, leaving the door wide open, anxious to hear what was going on downstairs. The shouts and laughter and dirty jokes of my old man and his mates went on until around half-past eleven. Then I heard the door open, his friends fall out of it, start up their cars and leave. I heard my old man mutter something to himself then swear at my mum, telling her to clean up the mess and come to bed. He said some other stuff, too, which I won't repeat because the thought of it still makes me sick to my stomach.

I lay down on my bed and shut my eyes, listening to the sound of my mum in the kitchen, washing dishes and drying them away. Suddenly, I heard the sound of my old man's heavy footsteps echoing in the stairway. I got up quickly, my heart beginning to beat faster, pushed my bedroom door closed, turned off my light and got back into bed, right under the covers.

My dad walked past my room and I heard him stop and listen through my door, his breath heavy. He pushed open the door to check on me, but he didn't come into the room. Instead, he shut the door and went to the bathroom, leaving me gulping in air, scared of what he might do next. Hoping that he would leave my mum alone. The bathroom door closed and I heard him fart loudly.

He finished up and headed for his own bedroom, shouting down to my mum, 'Hurry up! How long can it take, bitch?'

I removed the covers and sat up, fuming. I wanted to run out and shove him over the banister, down the stairs. I wanted to kick him and hit him and smash his face, but I was scared of him and I wasn't strong enough to hurt him.

So I lay there and listened, as I had done on so many other nights. Listened as my mum trudged reluctantly up the stairs and into the bathroom. Listened as she sobbed silently to herself. Listened as she crept slowly to their bedroom. I heard him call her crude names. Heard him slap her and push her down. Heard his panting and his breathing and . . .

I stood up, choking and trying to hold back the vomit. I ran out of my room and downstairs into the kitchen. I poured myself a glass of water and sat down on the floor in the dark, with my knees pulled up and my arms around them, crying silently. The noises that I had come to know as the nocturnal soundtrack of our house were muffled and distant. I heard my mother cry in pain at one point and all I could do was sit and sob like a child. I couldn't help her, I wasn't brave enough. I was a failure – that's how I saw myself. A coward. A baby. How could I have let him do that to her? How could I just sit there and listen and do nothing?

And that's when I heard *him* cry out in pain, cursing and swearing, and my mum run from their room.

I stood up and walked to the kitchen door, opening it. My mum was half-falling down the stairs, screaming, with my old man in pursuit. As she reached the bottom of the stairs, he caught her with a fist and she fell awkwardly on to the cold linoleum floor of the hallway. I wanted to help her, but I stayed in my hiding place, in the shadows, as my dad stood over her, swearing. He kicked her. Then again. Over and over. In her ribs, her back, her legs. She curled into a ball to try and deflect his blows, but he kept on, not letting up.

I turned and saw a half-empty bottle of whisky sitting on the worktop. I picked it up and walked through to the hall, my anger rising until I could think of nothing, see nothing, but my old man. Just him. Hitting my mum. Swearing at her.

In a rage, I swung the bottle above my head and brought it crashing down on to his skull. The bottle shattered, cutting into my hands, but I didn't feel it. I was numb. My dad staggered sideways, blood pouring from a wound in his head. He turned, looked at me in surprise, then caught me full in the face with a punch. Bone and cartilage cracked and splintered as my nose broke.

I hit the floor, my head spinning, and watched helplessly as he dragged my mum by her hair into the living room.

She was screaming again. I tried to move, but my legs had turned to jelly. I couldn't stand up. There was a banging at the front door and the sound of neighbours' voices shouting. I couldn't make out what they were saying. I was too busy concentrating on crawling to the kitchen. I pulled myself to my feet, still reeling from the punch, blinking back tears as I heard my mum's screams. I looked around for something to hurt him with. Anything. I wanted to kill him. I *wanted* to.

A heavy skillet came into view, hanging from a rack of pans. It was the one that my mum used to make paratha – like stuffed chapattis – which were my old man's favourites. I grabbed it and took it with me, slowly, into the living room. My mum was on the floor with her top ripped open and blood pouring from cuts to her face and head. There was already bruising around her eyes. My dad stood over her, his back to me. In his rage he was oblivious to me. I staggered over to him and used both hands to raise the heavy, cast-iron pan. Just as I brought it down, my mum's eyes widened as she saw me. My dad saw her eyes, caught the look of fear. He began to turn.

The pan caught him half into his turn. The sound of metal against flesh made me sick. I dropped the skillet and fell to my knees, retching. My dad fell to the side, landing on my mum. She screamed and pushed him off, before sitting up and crawling over to me. She kept on saying, 'Oh my God, Oh my God', in Punjabi. I couldn't look at my old man, not for a while. When I eventually did, he had fallen on his back, a huge gash in the side of his head. His eyes stared straight at me, even though they were dead. There was a look of surprise on his face.

You know the rest. The neighbours called the police. When they broke down the door they found me and my mum crying in the hallway, and my dad dead in the living room. My mum took all the blame for it – she made me tell the police that she had done it. Delivered the final blow. The one that killed him. She took all the blame and all the punishment, and the courts locked her away for murder. At the trial she pleaded self-defence, telling the jury that my dad would have killed us both if she hadn't acted. Only it's almost impossible to plead self-defence in this country. And the jury ignored her.

My dad's brothers gave testimony against my mum, telling the court about what a wonderful family man he had been and how much he had loved and lived for his wife and children. It was all lies. My uncles can't have failed to notice the black eyes and bruises that my mum had carried for nearly all twenty years of her marriage. Didn't they once stop to think how badly it had affected Balbinder and Harpal? Didn't they care? To them it was all about *izzat*, family honour, and we were not going to get in the way of that, no matter what that monster put us through.

We were forgotten by my dad's family after the trial and my mum's life sentence. It was down to my Uncle Harinder to start the appeal procedure to get my mum's sentence reduced. I think the lawyers were calling for 'diminished responsibility' or something. Only I knew different. My mum had no responsibility for it. It was me. I did it all. And, just as I had done with the beatings over the years, I hid the truth and let my mum bear the brunt. Not any more, though. I've told the police and the social workers and I'm telling you. I killed my old man. If anyone deserves to be in prison it is me and not her. There is to be a new trial because of what I've admitted. I'm going to plead guilty and tell the jury exactly what I've told you today. If they want to send me down then I don't care.

Remorse? No, I don't feel that at all. Why should I? It was us or him. I mean, do you really think that I wanted to kill my own father? Do you think that I want to be known as some psychological freak that you can write books about and teach courses on? I'm not a nutter. I'm not mad. I just had to stop him. He would have killed my mum and he would have killed me. And, like I said to my mum on my last visit to her prison, I would rather she visited me in a cell than at a gravestone. I'm sixteen now and I have had to become a man, for the sake of my younger brother and sister. I don't do all the normal teenage stuff like going out with girls and getting drunk – I can't. And I can't let my mum stay in prison for something that I did. I can't.

'And that is exactly what happened?' asked Dr Khan.

Ranjit wiped a tear from his eye and looked out of the window once more.

'Yes,' he whispered. 'That's what happened.'

Rukhsana Ahmad

Rukhsana Ahmad was born in Karachi and went to school in various cities in Pakistan, hating having to move so often, until her father retired and the family came back to settle in Karachi. She was thrilled when the university offered her a lectureship the year she completed her studies, but she gave up this post when she got married and came to live in London, where she has lived ever since – much longer than in any other city.

For several years now Rukhsana has freelanced as a writer. She has written many short stories and plays for the stage and radio. More recently she has written screenplays. She has always loved Urdu literature and is proud to have translated some fine poetry by women, as well as a novel. Her own first novel, *The Hope Chest*, tells the story of three young women grappling with the complicated business of growing up.

Rukhsana has dedicated 'First Love' to her brother, Rashid.

First Love

Rukhsana Ahmad

7 June 1995

Dear Diary,

Life isn't fair! I've got to say it again. Life isn't fair *at all*, is it? If it was, I know my hair wouldn't be such a dull wispy brown and my lips wouldn't be this awful purple-dark colour. And I would be a B cup by now. Everyone else I know is – well, everyone except Chandra, who is probably a C.

I don't think he even noticed I was there.

Not that I had a chance with the sort of introduction Rafi threw over his shoulder – 'My kid sister' – as if chucking more than a glance in my direction would be a waste of his smart new friend's time. How rude is that? Not even bothering to give us each other's names! Took me a while to work out his name: Feroze. Classy name, I thought.

Hardly surprising all I got from the hotshot was a quick flick of the eyebrows, one look, and half a smile. He didn't bother to stretch his lips all the way and I never saw the colour of his teeth. Nor of his eyes. I tried on my best 'See if I care' look, not sorry to have the chance to take in all his vital statistics. Such a contrast they were, the two of them together, like Laurel and Hardy, like Little and Large.

For one thing, he's nearly six feet tall. Whereas my brother Rafi, who likes to think he is a person of medium height, is quite short really, if only he faced up to it. He started trying when he was fourteen. Looping round a trapeze for forty minutes every single morning, drinking milk by the gallon, jogging endlessly, and then measuring his height week in, week out, for at least three years in a row. He's desperate to make the minimum for the air force and, who knows, with some luck he might just scrape in now.

I reckon it's hard to be a boy, sometimes. I must say, you wouldn't catch me doing all that just to gain an inch or two. To be fair, my friends always say he has his points: dark, almond eyes and thick gleaming hair, black as soot and dead straight. It's the kind of hair that suits a round face. I'd have loved it myself.

But as far as good looks go, this Feroze is hard to beat. I felt positively jealous of the waves of corkscrew curls cascading down to his shoulders, not to mention the perfect oval face. (We are all cursed with utterly round moon faces in our family, each and every one of us!) But the thing that really blew me away was his glorious golden colouring. *So-oo* Shahrukh Khan! I could almost feel the same sort of hum of energy rippling round him like a magical aura.

I hovered for a bit, staring at him, looking for an opening to slip into their debate. They were talking cricket scores – not regular stuff, mind you. I can always pitch into a conversation about how England would score against Sri Lanka or India or Pakistan – whoever they might be playing just then. But no, it was nothing so simple – it was all straight from Wisden. Best scores over the last century. As if anyone cares what Ranjit scored in 1918, or whenever the old geezer lived and played! Boys can be so pedantic when they're not being silly monkeys. They were both listening hard to each other then pitching straight in, racing to speak first. I really didn't have a chance. After a couple of open-mouthed 'er . . . er . . .' interruptions, I gave up.

Probably Feroze has an edge over Rafi, I started thinking to myself, secretly impressed. Rafi is absolutely the tops when it comes to crossword puzzles and quizzes, games and game shows – even the hard ones, the kind they do on telly. *Mastermind* or *Brain of the Century* – you name it, he can flow with it. If anything he's a jump ahead.

But before I could wriggle my way into their debate I heard my grandad's key in the door and I made myself scarce. Normally I recognize the sound of his shuffle as he plonks his bags on the doorstep before putting his key into the lock. I do think it's best to get out of his way at that time. Anyway, I know he is never pleased to see me sitting around with the boys. No point in risking a snub.

'There's no real harm in him, he just has a short-fuse problem.' Maa is always quick to rise to his defence. To tell you the truth, that's not a lot of help. I mean, if you have a friend over and they see your grandad having a go at you they're going to think the worst. They're not going to know all about him being a nice enough chap who's slightly hard of hearing and just has 'a short-fuse problem', are they?

I've tried to tell Maa this, but she always manages to miss the point.

Thank goodness Rafi understands. True he won't get drawn into a big discussion about Dada, but he does flash me a smile across the room, or he gives me one of his 'I know exactly what you mean' looks. It's comforting, that is. Over and above the undeniable perk of having a Shahrukh Khan lookalike drop by, I must admit, there are moments in your life when you're glad to have an older brother. It's certainly miles better than having a younger one, judging by my kid brother, Shafi. This afternoon, for example, he pounced on to the chair I vacated and occupied it so fast that I nearly whacked him.

Alarm bells rang for Rafi too, with Dada's entrance. First he tried to get Feroze to go up to his bedroom, then out into the conservatory, but when he didn't succeed in budging him from the scene he did the next best thing: sent him packing. He'd die rather than admit it, but I could tell he too was inwardly worried about Dada saying something offensive or humiliating in front of Feroze. He does have an alarming talent for doing both, Dada does.

Not that he means to, Maa reminds us: 'Don't forget, he was raised differently from you lot here! Bristol is a long way from Sialkot.' I catch Rafi roll up his eyes and give up. How different an upbringing allows you to be so difficult, sorry, different? I ask myself. I don't say it aloud though. If I did, Maa would just frown and ignore the question, as she tends to.

What if something embarrassing should happen in front of someone like Feroze? Imagine! Scary thought, isn't it? I wonder when Rafi will ask him back to the house again.

2 July 1995

Dear Diary,

Feels like ages since Feroze came to our house for the first time. But from the dates here I can see that in reality it's only a month. It's been a very long month though. One in which I've understood what they mean by the term 'learning curve'. I've learned everything, almost everything, there is to know about Feroze, and loads about falling for someone.

I know what colours he likes, what foods, which football club he supports and which cricket team. I know his favourite bands, his favourite single, his best sports hero, the kind of films he watches, the books he reads, where he goes for a swim and even where he goes for haircuts. I am virtually an encyclopedia of information about Feroze Sethna, aka Fizz. I know the history of the Sethnas: how clannish they are, what they believe in, where exactly in the world they come from, what language they speak, et cetera, et cetera, et cetera. Try me on anything, and I'll know the answers. I reckon I know a lot more than his latest friend, my brother Rafi.

In fact, Rafi might wonder how I know so much? To tell you the truth, I myself am impressed with how much I've found out in so little time through a combination of sound detective work and careful mental notes. I made friends with his younger sister, Honey, who thinks the world of him. She is quite easily triggered into talking about him. I just have to mention Fizz and, knowing my dedication as a listener, she rambles through a catalogue of his comments and activities. I just sit there entranced, lapping it up, storing it all in my memory as if my life depends on it.

What good this information will do me only God knows since He alone can look into the future. My secret hope is that one day all this knowledge will help me find a way into her brother's favour, somehow.

I hang out where I know it's at least possible to catch a glimpse of him. Outside Malorees Sixth Form College, at the bus stop, around the playing fields, as near his house as I dare. Surprisingly, I haven't seen him much, given the amount of time I have invested in hanging out at the most likely spots. Idiot that I am, every time I see him my mouth feels dry, my knees wobble and I feel a weird sensation in the pit of my belly – a strange mixture of excitement and fear. A part of me is dying to get near him, to touch him, whilst a part of me wants to run a mile. No one else I know has affected me quite like this. Honestly, I've never felt anything like this before.

5 July 1995

Dear Diary,

Woke up this morning to the perfume of joss sticks and a quiet hum of prayers hanging in the air. In a split second I remembered. The truth is, I had remembered last night. It's my dad's anniversary today – the ninth if my maths is up to it, so I do know the routine. My mum says her prayers early in the morning, then organizes food to be sent to the mosque in his name before she leaves for the hospital. I've never worked out what time she wakes up to be able to cook. The very thought of it makes me feel tired. I turned over to block out the memory and the sensations, not quite ready to face the morning.

Long after she's gone Dada just sits there, with a large

handkerchief, praying, wiping his eyes every now and then, and blowing his nose, as he prepares himself to take the food over to the mosque. I watch him sniffing, grieving, like an old woman, not caring how he looks. His tears crawl slowly into his grey beard and I do feel sorry for him, but the fine trickle that runs fitfully from his nose grosses me out a little, so I don't hug him.

Sometimes I think my dad is quite lucky to have died so young. He'll always look as handsome and fit and well as he does in the photograph on the mantelshelf in our lounge, even though he had a tricky heart. A heart that let him down one day at work – just when he was supposed to be helping another sick man get to the hospital. He was a paramedic, my dad, and he was out with an ambulance that day. The patient survived; he didn't. That's the way it goes sometimes.

My mother tells that story with a wistful look in her eyes – as if life and death are simply a matter of short straws and long ones, and that was just an evil moment, when my poor dad picked the wrong one. I suppose she cannot accept that that was his allotted time to join his Maker. Maybe she suspects that Death played a cruel ironic joke, or that Death took him completely by accident in a momentary confusion about *who* was really meant to die: the eighty-five-year-old the crew had gone to rescue, or poor Papa who had never been ill in his thirty-five years.

Dada reckons it's all written up somewhere, in a Book of Destiny. For him it's a tragedy that was cast in stone by some secret power long before my dad was born. A tragedy for which my father was not responsible in the least and to which he could not have contributed. It annoys Dada no end when Rafi goes on about eating healthily and exercising to avoid heart disease. Death is a fact of life, he'll say, with that serious solemn air that older people use to lend weight to the scrappiest of thoughts or any old saying they can muster. If you take them at face value and dive into the meaning you hit rock-bottom a lot sooner than you expected to.

I stayed in bed, pretending to be asleep. I couldn't face a debate about Destiny first thing in the morning. It scares me a little, a day like this, because it makes me think about us dying – even if it is quite far into the future: first the 'Olds', then Rafi, me, then Shafi, but worst of all Feroze. Doesn't bear thinking about, does it? Buried, six feet below ground, with the creepy-crawlies and dead roots.

She touched my forehead gently. 'Shah Bano! You'll be late for school, if you don't get up now.'

I screwed my eyes against the glare of the bare bulb and squinted at Maa's face. Her eyes were red and so was the fine tip of her nose. She was dressed in white. No lipstick. Those are her rules for the anniversary. I buried my head back in the pillow with a grunt. Life's not easy, is it? I thought. How I hate getting out of bed.

'Do you still miss him?' I asked her, when she tried to pull the quilt away from my face ten minutes later.

'Mmm . . .' she murmured vaguely, nodding her head both ways. I wasn't sure whether that was a 'yes' or a 'no', or if she meant both. She never talks about it – certainly never to any of us, anyway.

'Get up, you'll be late!' she said, in her early-morning-crisp no-nonsense tone. I could see the shutters fall in my face as she disappeared downstairs, racing against time, to get organized for work.

I do realize it's quite a taxing job, being an appointments

secretary in a busy county hospital. They offered her the post soon after my father's death – a very good thing for all of us. We needed the income *and* she is glad to get out of the house, she always insists.

On the way back from school I decided to stay on the bus right up to the last stop. A ten-minute walk from there takes you to the cemetery. It was the first time I went on my own. The plants round the grave had been watered and there were fresh flowers by the headstone. I wondered who had been to visit. Was it Maa or Dada?

The attendant came round to the grave with an air of bustle and an overflowing can of water. A ruddy man with dusty red hair, he has the muddiest boots and the broadest wrists I've ever seen, with a scar spiralling round the left one. He poured more water on to the plants. I stood feeling awkward and a bit guilty. This is a moment that usually prompts my mother to put her hand in her bag and pull out a note, which she discreetly slips to him.

My fingers clung to the pound coin inside my coat pocket. I worried that it was not enough for a tip. 'Your brother's given me something already,' he said, as if he'd guessed my thoughts. Although his tone was easy and comforting I could feel myself blushing. Aha! I thought. Rafi comes by himself too.

He gave me the slightest of smiles, the best you'd get in a cemetery, to reward me for coming to visit my dad's grave, then vanished as quickly and quietly as he had come, leaving me to communicate with Papa in private.

I waited a moment after he'd gone before I turned to talk to Papa about things in earnest. That was my plan. Talk to him – about my life, about the future, about my choice of A levels, about Feroze – about all those things that I keep meaning to bring up with Maa and never manage to. Perhaps she's too busy to stop and listen, or perhaps I'm too scared or too shy. Maybe he'll give me some advice, send me some inspiration, I thought.

Muttering a prayer to myself, I knelt down, my right hand on the grave, my left one on my heart, and shut my eyes to get closer to him. Closer. Desperate to feel something, anything. Graves can open, spirits can walk. I knew something was bound to happen. For a moment nothing did and then, suddenly, I felt a drop in temperature, an odd chill in the air. I shivered and opened my eyes. A fluffy grey cloud loafed across the sun, casting a shadow over everything.

Directly in front of me was the familiar gravestone with the faded prayer in Arabic. Words that I had read over the years and Dada had interpreted for me time and again: *He alone is the Maker of all the Universes. He, Who is indifferent, Who is not born of anyone, nor has given birth to anyone. He rules supreme and knows every secret, that which is hidden and that which is manifest.*

I gripped the stone, trying to take comfort in its warmth. The message bore a new meaning for me in that moment. It calmed me in a funny kind of way. As if Papa was telling me not to look too far ahead, that seeking knowledge of the future before events unfold in the fullness of time was a kind of impertinence on my part. I turned round and left the cemetery by the nearest gate, determined I would not tell anyone about my visit to Papa's grave – at least not today.

Finally, the bus trundled along. Only twenty minutes later than its scheduled time – not bad for that route. Banks of clouds had assembled with impressive speed to frown the warm afternoon sunshine away. Their dark rim round the sun made me feel anxious once again.

Perhaps I should not expect too much of the future, I thought as I got on the bus. With some luck I might get the grades I need to pick the A-level options I want; but to have all that *and* the hero of my dreams as well adds up to an embarrassing share of the goodies. Just a little too ambitious, or is the word 'greedy'? I dropped a pound coin into the slot machine, pulled off the ticket it spat out and stumbled blindly towards an empty seat, telling myself, 'No one has that much luck – not real people, in real life, surely.'

Don't they, ever? I had to bite my tongue almost at once. There he was, sat right next to the empty seat I had picked, large as life, real as the smell of diesel and the purr of vibrations rippling through the bus. He blanked me for just a tick before he recognized me. Instantly his eyes sent out the warmest rays of sunshine, a brilliant scorcher of a smile that dazzled me, lifting my spirits straight up to the sky. My heart tripped, my knees gave way and I landed inelegantly into the empty seat next to him.

'Where are *you* coming from, Sugar Puff?' he asked in a gruff big-brother voice, using the pet name Rafi uses for me sometimes. I cringed inwardly, ignoring the dig in that name, and tried to smile as coyly as I dared. Waste of time, I suspect. I don't think he took in my mumbled reply. Most probably he believed me because he didn't notice the detail of my answer.

'The deed's done,' he said somewhat mysteriously as I sat there chewing my lips, clenching and unclenching my fingers nervously. I looked at him, flummoxed, not at all sure what he meant by that. He paused, giving me time to catch up, but although I smiled at him brightly I had no idea what he was talking about.

'We've submitted our applications today, Rafi and I,' he said, and then, as I continued to look blank, he added helpfully, 'for the air force.'

That *was* a bit unexpected. 'Already?' was all I could muster.

'Didn't Rafi tell you he was going to apply?' he asked, as if my lack of knowledge was a sign that I was mentally deficient besides being unworthy of secrets.

'He did, sort of,' I lied bravely.

It suddenly made sense, Rafi's visit to Papa's grave. He was making big decisions too.

In a way it is not such a surprise. Papa's older brother, my Uncle Safdar, has always said what a great career it is for a bright young man. He saw action as a communications officer with the Royal Air Force in the Falklands War – must be the only Paki in the whole of Bristol who did. Though he retired last year, he has some amazing stories to tell about the RAF. The trouble is, all his life Uncle Saf has admired the flyers in the force much more than the signals men. They are the bee's knees, or the cat's whiskers, whatever you prefer. Rafi hangs out at their place often enough, so he is steeped in the same admiration and respect for pilots.

Lately, he seems obsessed with aircrafts and flying. Giant posters of warplanes from every decade since the First World War hug his walls. He is forever buying paperbacks of Second World War novels and histories of battles from second-hand bookshops, and he subscribes to two defence magazines.

He knows countless stories of war heroes and dogfights,

Spitfires and bombers. Only yesterday I caught him reading *Reach for the Sky* for the third time this year. When he's not talking about heroism and valour he's giving us tech specs for Harriers and Jaguars, MiGs and Tornadoes. I listen, pretending to be more interested than I am. Everything jumbles together and gets dreadfully mixed up in my memory: names, planes, years and times. Increasingly, he talks to Shafi rather than me about his passion, since I tend to resist and even openly object to it at times.

Maa is not too keen on this RAF career either, so I am not surprised Rafi had kept his application so quiet. It made sense for him to do that till it became totally unavoidable.

'There's your stop, Sugar Puff.' Feroze flicked my plait in a playful gesture that was annoyingly like something Rafi might do.

Cheeky devil, I thought. Tears stung my eyes at this final humiliation. It made me feel like I was five. I grabbed my stuff and dashed off, waving a quick goodbye, terrified he might see my tears and guess how I feel about him.

I got my revenge on him and Rafi, though, by letting their little secret out into the light of day, over dinner tonight. You should have seen Rafi's face. Hmmmmm!

10 August 1995

Dear Diary,

Looking back on the bus ride, I suppose it needn't have felt like such a stroke of luck to see him there. Every single word he said, every single look, and every single gesture was utterly patronizing. Clearly he sees me both as his friend's kid sister and as his kid sister's friend. Either way, I am a child in his eyes, and all I can do is pray hard that I grow up quickly to catch up with him. Hopefully before the acceptance of their applications from the RAF comes through.

Secretly I wonder if they take Pakis in jobs like that. But I don't want to ask Rafi or Feroze. I know what they'd say. 'You need to watch that great big chip on your shoulder, poppet.' That is Rafi, in denial, as usual.

'We live in a more humane society than the rest of the world. There might be a handful of racists, but you'd get those in Turkey or Timbuktu, in India or Pakistan, wherever you go. I don't think there is any discrimination here, not in the least!' That's Feroze, even stronger in defence of Queen and country.

Except Hassan wouldn't agree. He reckons there is discrimination against the likes of us wherever we go. When we lived in Moulton Road, in the grim and grimy terrace where all of us were born, Hassan's family lived right next door. He and Zahid still run a youth club down there, in the poorest end of Bristol. He came round today to see us, but Rafi behaved as if he was only my guest, not his, and Hassan seemed happy enough talking to me. I like the sound of his gentle voice and the way his eyes darken with intensity when he's thinking.

I find it so much easier talking to him because we agree about more things than not. Whereas when I talk to Feroze we argue about more things than not.

Perhaps I should care less about good looks than I do. So what if Hassan isn't quite the challenge to Shahrukh Khan? At least he knows who SK is. And he's studying medicine, not learning to fight. But will my silly heart ever listen?

Turns out Hassan had come to ask Rafi and Feroze if

they might help him build attendance at his youth club. Perhaps get the lads into playing cricket or footy? Both of them said they were far too busy with studies and stuff. Busy? Scared, more like, I thought. They find Moulton Road a bit rough now. I don't think they could manage the sort of wild bunch you'd get down that end of town.

I suppose they're both too polite to be completely honest with Hassan. It's hard, isn't it? White lies make a lot of sense sometimes.

I have an uncomfortable feeling Hassan saw through them. He said nothing, just smiled, and asked them to *at least try*. His eyes are sad, as if they see the distance between us and the kids we used to be, down in Moulton Road.

I wouldn't say it to Rafi and Feroze, but in my heart I think it would be brilliant if they don't get into the RAF at all. Neither of the two of them. I'd hate to think of them chucking bombs from a height of several thousand metres on real cities full of real people. What if they hit them, even just a few of them, killing real people that they never meant to kill? Blowing them to smithereens. Awful thought, isn't it?

5 July 1996

Dear Diary,

Papa's anniversary again!

I'm so glad the term is over. What a long hard slog it's been! Who'd have thought it would feel so long without Rafi? Maa was really worried about his going off to the RAF. So was I, for reasons of my own, but I don't think Shafi gave it much thought.

She is always full of absurd fears; I suppose Papa's death has made her quite insecure. She imagines the worst if one of us is late. Every night our return home is a kind of triumph, a huge relief for her, as if we were away on a high-risk mission. She sleeps better, she says, once we're all back and safely tucked in bed. (Personally, I've always seen this as her very own excuse for absurdly early curfew times!) She's finding it very hard that he's chosen a career that has taken him right out of the safety of this home so early.

You can see her struggle with his absence. Her prayers are endlessly long. She sits there for hours with her rosary, eyes shut, lips moving, face filled with intensity.

As the summer rolled on we noticed his absence more. I realized for the first time how much he helps to smooth over tricky situations at home. Somehow he has the knack for defusing that dangerous tetchy moment – when Dada is about to explode! I imagine Rafi saves up a hoard of goodies so he can trot one out to save his skin, or mine, or Shafi's – even Maa's at times. His success stories, his exam results, or his sports prizes; sometimes it's just a little anec-dote about a cricket hero – anything to counter those difficult moments. We've all been saved by one of his charmers.

To make matters worse, Dada has been picking on poor Maa much more, specially when he isn't picking on one of us. Nothing Maa did today was right: too much salt in the rice, too little meat in the curry; he could see she was wasting milk, then it was Fairy Liquid, then electricity; and, worst of all, she'd bought the wrong brand of margarine. All that in one day! I cursed myself for not being ready with a single joke, or a story that might help defuse the situation.

Without a doubt Rafi's absence has been a strain. Both Shafi and I are quite weary. Not Maa. She just smiles calmly and turns to her rosary, as if that's the answer to every problem in her life, and I wonder what she makes of Dada's bad temper, his constant bad humour with her. 'His rheumatism is troubling him,' she offers as a lame excuse in his defence every time he behaves abominably.

Next week Rafi and Feroze should both set off from the RAF base for their summer break. That's when their holidays begin. Not a day too soon. It will be utter bliss to have them here at home. I can't wait to have Rafi back here – and to see Feroze. Well, at least whilst he is in town there's always hope.

15 August 1996

Dear Diary,

It's amazing to see how changed they both are after just six months as cadets. They both look bigger and heftier and more brown. They speak more slowly, as if what they say carries more weight and must be heard, and they both move sedately like grown-ups. They look less like boys and more like men than they did before they left.

Rafi asks fewer questions than he used to and calmly delivers opinions about everything; his confidence has grown enormously. The good news is, he's been picked for flying. *How lucky to have your dream come true!* It's obvious that pilots are the kings in their world, the cream of the officer class. You can tell from the way Feroze watches him and listens to him now, with a hint of respect.

Not that Feroze is unhappy with his own entry into aeronautics engineering. He does love his work, and I feel it's that bit better if he's not flying those wretched planes. To me he looks more gorgeous than ever. Shahrukh Khan, eat your heart out!

'Do *you* get the heebie-jeebies too, Maa, when Rafi talks about warplanes that drop tons of bombs on people?' I asked her today as I was helping her dry dishes.

'Yes, I do,' she murmured. I could see her turning pages in her head, remembering. She speaks slowly, dredging up memories. 'They are just . . . terrifying. When Pakistan was at war with India our house was right next to the army's headquarters. When the air-raid sirens wailed in the middle of the night we took shelter in a trench that was halfway between the barbed wire of its perimeter and the front of our house. There's nothing worse than waiting in the dark, on the ground below, wondering *where* a plane will shed its load and *on whom*? We read about "the casualties" in the papers the next day with a mixture of guilt and awe. Isn't it sad, close to the end of the twentieth century we're just a tiny bit better at saving lives, but we've got a whole lot better at destroying them?'

Mrs Rose, our English teacher, jabs her finger in the air to make the same point more emphatically. 'War?' she says. 'They can say what they like, but it's never clean, never fair, never without a cost.' She talks about the lunacy of war till the class begins to yawn. I wish I could tell her to stop in time. There is a perfect moment, when we're all listening and almost agree with her. But then she goes on a tad too long and loses half the class. She is full of stories of the peace marches, and the camp at Greenham in the eighties where she was the lookout and shopper-in-chief for three weekends running.

'The point that Gulliver makes with the wars of the

Lilliputians . . .' she says, taking a deep breath, forgetting she is repeating herself. By that time, very few of us in the class are listening to her and, to everyone's relief, the bell goes. Yet her lesson about the point that Gulliver made is etched on to my mind forever, and for good reason.

I imagine stories of war and death locked together in a gruesome embrace. I hate them both quite definitely. Just when I was doing my summer project last year about the Lilliputians' war in *Gulliver's Travels*, images of NATO planes bombing the former Yugoslavia dominated our television screens and made me feel quite ill. I couldn't help thinking of the people on the ground, in schools and hospitals, shops and playgrounds, with a shudder.

Feroze comes round almost every day – as if they don't see enough of each other at the base. It sounds really tough, being a cadet. The number of people who have power over you, who'll punish you, tease you, bully you in the name of training is not something I'd want to face. It seems monstrously harsh – the lifestyle, the training, the work. They say it toughens you up, prepares you for the job. You can't be a wimp; that's the ultimate cuss in their world. Why anyone would want to stay and carry on training in spite of such harsh treatment really beats me. But here are two people thrilled to be part of that exclusive club, the Royal Air Force. They go round with its motto emblazoned on their hearts: RISE ABOVE THE REST! I am impressed with their loyalty.

I tease them, though, about why they have to rise above the rest. To wreck and kill, bomb and destroy. Rafi is unabashed. 'Might sound extreme in peace time; it's absolutely essential for survival in a war situation.' I ignore his defence and walk off haughtily.

Hassan came too today, to catch up with Rafi. I made us some coffee and joined them. Soon I caught a despairing look in Hassan's eyes. We both feel well out of it.

The two of them use the lingo from that world, constantly talking about people we don't know, with nasty nicknames like Longjohn Peter, Fatlips Forbes, Squeak and, worst of all, Cheesy Toes. None of their course mates have flattering pet names. So far I've not been able to extract their official nicknames from them. They just smile coyly and refuse to tell. So laddish, this deep loyalty and bond of affection that's grown between them!

Eventually, Rafi remembers that Hassan is there too and asks about Zahid. Both of them are agog when Hassan tells us he's somewhere in Mirpur or Afghanistan, training to fight.

'Fight!' Rafi exclaims.

'Where?' Feroze asks cautiously, exchanging a look with Rafi.

'Dunno? I think . . . Chechnya, perhaps?' Hassan looks at me, defensively, adding they are no longer in touch. An awkward moment of silence lurks around us, and Hassan gets up to leave. No one asks him to stay a bit more. He hastens, sensing his stay could have been shorter. I feel a bit sorry for him, but I can understand the awkwardness. I mean, it is hard when friendships go peculiar, as they do sometimes. I wish they wouldn't!

I suppose I shouldn't complain. Rafi and Feroze are both more courteous to me now than they used to be. They treat me more like a person, almost a grown-up, which is great.

Late into the night we sat chatting, smoking cigs; they both had sneaky bottles of beer under the bed, I had a cappuccino. I tried to talk about Hassan, to see how they felt about him, but they kept going back to Zahid. How strange that he should go off, like some weird missionary, risking life and limb in someone else's war! Wasn't it amazing, the reach of the Fundoos, right into the heart of England, in schools of medicine and computer sciences of all places?

Their sneering feels uncomfortable, but I don't want to pick an argument with them when things are going so well between us. I resist the temptation to quote Mrs Rose again – pacifism is a dirty word in their book. I decide not to say what Hassan might have said to defend Zahid, and watch Feroze instead. He pays a bit more attention to my nervous little comments than he has ever done before, or so I imagine. Once, when Rafi was talking, I even caught him looking at me – just a glance, but it made my heart flutter.

Perhaps things are changing for me, after all, in the right direction? Who knows what it will be like when they return home for Christmas? If I'm lucky I'll be checking out universities then.

3 July 1997

Dear Diary,

I must confess there's *something* about men in uniforms that's hard to resist. One and all, they looked splendid on the day they were commissioned. Only two people could attend, so Uncle Safdar went with Maa. They disgraced themselves by breaking into tears – when Rafi's wings were pinned to his chest – for poor Papa who could not be there. Rafi was still as a statue. He stepped back, saluted and spun round to return to his position in a flawless salute, without a glance at anyone.

Feroze's dad had made a two-hour-long video of the entire passing-out parade, which he copied for Dada, Shafi and me. Rafi looked amazing; but when everyone had gone to bed, I played the videotape by myself, pausing it again and again to watch Feroze stamp his foot and spin round smartly after his salute. It made my heart jump, each time.

It is amazing to watch a bunch of boys, raw as reeds, knocked into shape in a very short span of time to deliver a show that has the polished perfection of a ballet company. Each movement of each cadet is precise, measured. Their faces glow with the long-awaited, pined-for magic of the moment when they shed their cadet inexperience forever and march confidently as officers into a career they adore.

I watch the passion, the fervour in their eyes, and I think of Mrs Rose and worry.

I relive a huge argument I had with the two of them during one of our late-night sessions last year. 'I've no guilt, no ambivalence about my job, Shah. Defence is absolutely central to the survival of a nation,' Rafi announces grandly, when I dwell on my horror of war and try preaching to them about the value of human life.

'It's an honourable profession, like medicine,' Feroze quickly pitches in to help Rafi. 'You prepare to fight, you prepare to die – killing is an unpleasant but necessary evil; an unfortunate part of the process, sometimes. If we're lucky, really lucky, we may never have to do it. Trouble is, in a way war and death connect almost like life and death. There's a logic, an inevitability – you wish it wasn't there, but it's unavoidable. It's part of the deal.'

'So glib and easy! I suppose they train you to think like

that.' I sneer and walk out, unable to express my views as clearly as both of them can.

Now they're commissioned. It's too late for us to debate all this and I sit there worrying: what if there is a war? I'd be terrified, Maa would be sleepless, and Dada would surely go to pieces and make life hell for all of us.

'Who knows what the future holds? With some luck, they'll draw salaries from the force and never go to war,' Mrs Rose said to comfort me the day I went in to say goodbye at the end of term and confess about Rafi.

I hope she's right. By the time I've brushed my teeth and got into bed I am much calmer. 'I should pray, like Maa does, every night,' I tell myself, but my eyes get heavy and my fingers too tired to scribble any more.

2 January 1998

Dear Diary,

This morning Maa sat beaming over her breakfast. She had a cheque from Rafi laid out on the table next to her bowl of cereal.

'Two hundred pounds!' she said, looking up. 'He wants me to buy myself a new sari. Why would anyone want to spend two hundred pounds on one sari? Generous, isn't he, like his father?' Her voice softened with the memory.

He is, I thought. I opened his letter to me. He'd sent fifty each to Shafi and me. Maa is convinced there isn't a sari good enough for his money and I expect she's right.

He sent Dada a woollen scarf, knowing he won't accept money from him. Dada is chuffed, but has a strange way of showing it. He grunts and moans, as always. 'How long have I got to live? Throwing money on a cashmere scarf for

167

an old man! He must have paid so much for this, the young fool. What a waste!'

We rang him before going to bed tonight, to say thank you. He was dismissive, casual, as if none of it was a big deal. But I could tell how thrilled he was to be able to send that kind of money, now that he has his flying allowance as a pilot.

I felt proud of him in that moment, despite the fact that he has to fly warplanes. Hopefully Mrs Rose is right and he'll never be sent on bombing missions. Never have to kill for a living.

Secretly I wonder if Feroze has sent any gifts to his family and if he is as generous as Rafi. A tiny hope creeps into my heart: maybe he'll send me something when he sends a gift to his little sister? There's little reason to imagine he will, but my stupid heart seldom listens to my brain.

20 August 1998

Dear Diary,

This evening I phoned Rafi in the mess because Maa really wanted to speak to him, but they couldn't find him in there. The man who answered suggested we try the duty room. I waited on the line for a long while, then I heard a familiar voice, and my heart jumped. It was Feroze; someone had thought to fetch him instead.

'I'll get him to call you, soon as he comes back,' he said. 'He's gone for a drive with some friends. In fact, they might go for a drink and they could be very late, so don't wait up.'

I felt like chatting with him, just idle phone chit-chat, but he sounded a bit terse. That annoyed me. Too busy now he's an officer? Arrogant git!

'Rafi hasn't phoned, has he?' Maa asks, before going to bed.

'Feroze said he might be late, don't wait up. I'll wait, Maa. Go to sleep, you look tired.'

I meant it then – but I'm so knackered . . . I try and . . . I just can't keep my . . .

21 August 1998

Life isn't fair . . . at all.

27 August 1998

Dear Diary,

A week has gone by, and I still can't believe it. The whole day ticks through my head slowly: how it began and how it ended. I go over it again and again, just to make myself believe it. Each moment of that day is clear, and so vivid.

8:00 a.m. Maa is in the hall getting ready to leave. The phone rings and I rush to get it, leaving a splutter of cereal on the table.

'There he is now!' Maa's voice is full of relief as she comes in to listen.

It is Feroze again.

'Shah, is Auntie there? Please ask her to wait for me. I'm coming over; I'll be there very soon. Don't go out, please. We need to talk.' He sounds strange, remote and very serious, as if . . . there's a war on somewhere. My heart sinks and my hands become sweaty.

'Who is it, Shah? Was it Rafi? What is it?' Maa looks at me closely.

Her questions become shrill in my ear and confuse me. I shake my head. I'm not sure what his phone call means. I don't know what to say to her. Nothing in my life has prepared me for this.

But Maa is shaking like a leaf already. I touch her and realize her body is cold as ice, so cold it feels moist. I sit her down and bring her a cup of tea. It rattles in her hand, she can't swallow. She shakes her head, drawing away from the tea. I am terrified it will choke her and put the cup down.

I phone Shafi on his mobile and ask him to fetch Dada from the mosque on his way back home. Shafi arrives before Feroze, luckily. Only he hasn't been able to find Dada. Just as well, he says, as he comes and posts himself beside me, close to the window. We wait, avoiding each other's eyes – terrified of the worst, hoping for the best.

In the background I can hear Maa moaning in a low voice, like a sick animal.

I tell myself this will be like all those other times when she terrified herself needlessly because one of us was late and for a good reason. 'He's OK, he's got to be . . .' I repeat, unable to contemplate the worst; but I feel shaky too as I look out of the window.

It sounded like a mobile. What does 'soon' mean? How far are they now? How long have we got to wait? Will they come any minute now? Questions whizz through my head. I look again, but the road outside is empty.

'Don't be so scared, Maa! They're coming to see us, that doesn't mean nothing.' Shafi hugs Maa clumsily, concern written across his face.

'Please, Maa, don't worry so much. Maybe he's not well.

Pray, just pray. It *will* be good news.' I repeat the same sequence of phrases without the force of real conviction in my voice.

But she is not listening. She is moaning, muttering under her breath. 'It's too late. I should never have let him . . . I should not have . . . It's my fault. Too late now!'

Suddenly I hear Shafi's voice – trembling, husky, filled with doom. 'Shah! There's two of them! *Two?*' Reluctantly, he goes to open the door.

Maa and I follow him to the front room in silence.

Two men in uniforms enter our house. They're wearing dark glasses. Feroze is ahead of the other officer. He holds a peak cap, clutching it quite formally. They stand in the presence of the moment, respectful, aware of Maa's anguish. There is a curious hush in the room.

No one has told me, but I know what this means. Out of the blue, I remember the familiar words in Arabic: *He rules supreme and knows every secret, that which is hidden and that which is manifest.* In a cruel flash I see an empty grave.

From the corner of my eye I see Maa collapse. She slumps into the sofa, her hand on her heart as she struggles for air. Her breath comes in short spasms.

I can see Feroze is close to tears. He struggles to introduce the older man, Wing Commander Pearson, who speaks slowly with a tender, mournful note in his voice.

'Mrs Janjua, it is with great sadness that I must inform you . . .' His voice falls with each syllable, it becomes harder to hear him. I screech to drown out the sound. But he continues in his low, formal tone, '. . . there was a tragic incident at two-thirty p.m. yesterday. Rafi's plane crashed . . .' His voice fades to a murmur.

I wish he would shut up. All I want is news of Rafi. My

need to see him in the flesh grows with every passing second. *He's got to be all right*, I think . . . People survive crashes, don't they? 'How is he? How's Rafi?' I ask. 'Which hospital is he in?'

Wing Commander Pearson avoids my eyes. When he refuses to respond I decide to ignore him and tug at Feroze's sleeve, impatiently begging him for news. 'Why won't you tell me how he is, Feroze? *You've got to tell me.* Please tell me!' Feroze looks at me with silent pity in his eyes and a vague apology.

I hit him on his shoulder with my fists, desperate with anxiety, until he mouths the words slowly but clearly despite the quaver in his voice: 'He died, Shah, he died in the crash. He . . . is no more.'

I needed to hear it, I suppose – to believe it.

RAF Base Calgary
19 September 1998

Dear Shah,

I hope to join you and the family tomorrow to mark the end of the saddest month in our lives.

The hardest thing about being in the force must be to lose a friend. If it is your best friend you do have everyone's support and sympathy. They've all been very good to me this past month. That's the great thing about the RAF – the brotherhood, the feeling of kinship. Everyone cares about everyone else, as if they were family.

The pain of his loss continues in its intensity, despite the weeks gone by. It was the hardest thing I've had to deal with, ever. It is a tradition: the casualty's best friend has to accompany the commanding officer. So I was the one who had to present Rafi's peak cap to all of you. Forgive me for bringing such awful news. I'd have said no if I had the guts when they asked me to do it. As long as I live I hope I'll never have to do it again.

I remember feeling vague and numb, almost as if I were stuck in an awful nightmare. Each one of you seemed pale with shock, terrified, when we walked into the room.

You've asked for more details of the 'attempted' hijacking. They are emerging slowly. All we have at the moment is an imaginative reconstruction of what probably happened.

They think the intruder hid himself in the cockpit just before take-off. Everyone here believes Rafi showed amazing courage and professionalism – he did everything by the book. The control tower got the SOS, loud and clear: '166 being hijacked.' Then, once again, they read '166 being hijacked!' before they lost all radio contact.

His voice was a touch high, with a tiny chink of tension, but there was no hint of panic or fear. It was still clear, still rational. I've heard the tape a million times and wondered what *I* would have done.

It was a no-win situation. His first solo flight in a Harrier T10. It's a twin control, designed for teaching. The intruder was a fellow officer, a skilled pilot, senior to Rafi by six months. Only he was banned from flying earlier that week after he failed his annual psychological fitness tests. He'd become too dangerously unstable and suicidal to be allowed to fly any more, but he refused to accept that judgement.

He seized control of the plane as soon as they were airborne and was speeding straight towards station headquarters to avenge himself against the RAF. It was a crazy plan. He would have inflicted terrible damage and killed several officers – not just Rafi, who became the butt of his bitter rage because of his success.

It was impossible to beat him: a skilled opponent who came to avenge himself, *prepared to die*. Rafi probably never saw his face, but he tried hard to wrestle the controls back. At some point Rafi decided to match the stake rather than surrender. I suppose, for him, there was no other choice but to make the ultimate sacrifice in the course of duty. It was the only way to stop a near massacre. There were so many officers and men in the building; the aircraft crashed close to the perimeter of the headquarters. Although the investigation is still incomplete they have commended him for the highest military honour. No favours there! No one deserves it more.

I am so proud to be associated with him, but I do miss him very much. I guess for the family any award is small compensation for an irreparable loss. But please remember, it *mattered* to Rafi, he believed in the glory of the country. And so do I.

The crash must have happened soon after midday. Then that awful moment when you rang in the evening: every one at the base knew, but we weren't allowed to say a thing till the facts were verified and the next-of-kin informed by the base commander. *No one knew what to say to you.*

He was popular, believe you me. There were no cheery drunks at the bar that day, no music, no laughter. A pall of stunned silence hung over the base – truly deep sorrow for a lost colleague. It was a shock, a bitter reminder of the ultimate stake in our world.

Someone decided, God knows who, that I should take your call and cover his absence for a few hours. Just so you wouldn't keep ringing. The matter had to be processed and that would take time.

I heard your voice. To me, you sounded just like Honey. I felt awful lying to you. I can't even remember now what exactly I said, but I made up a story and finished as quickly as I could.

Then, I must confess, to my shame I sat down on the floor and wept like a baby, not caring that the others could see me.

Your loss has also been profoundly mine.

Ever yours,

Feroze

13 Moulton Road
Bristol
30 October 1998

My dear Shah Bano,

I heard. And I meant to write ages ago – just found it impossible to choose my words. Everything must sound trite. *So, so sorry.* I can only guess what you and your family are going through, especially your poor mum. I heard about the military honours and the award. Hope that helps a little – after all, Rafi believed in all that.

We had a minute's silence at the youth club, to remember him. Most of the lads here are amazed at his sacrifice. These choices are hard for them to understand. I heard someone whisper, 'What a shame! He had everything to live for.'

I hope you'll find some comfort in the fact that he was still utterly innocent. No blood on his hands, no cynicism in his heart, no disillusionment to sour the dream. I hope and pray you will all find peace, eventually.

Sadly yours,

Hassan

PS: Would love to see you, and the others, of course. Do call when you're up to a visit. Won't you?

Debjani Chatterjee

Debjani Chatterjee was born in India and came to Britain at nineteen. She has worked in the steel industry, education and community relations. She chairs the National Association of Writers in Education, contributes to the Poetry Society's 'poetryclass' and is a founder member of the Bengali Women's Support Group. Sheffield Hallam University gave her an honorary doctorate for 'outstanding contribution to literature and the arts and community service'.

Debjani has been called 'a voice of rare originality' (David Morley) and 'a poet full of wit and charm' (Andrew Motion). Her poetry has won major prizes. Award-winning anthologies include *Barbed Lines* and *The Redbeck Anthology of British South Asian Poetry*. Her many books for children include *Animal Antics* and *Rainbow World*. Her play *The Honoured Guest* was toured in schools by Twisting Yarn Theatre and is published by Faber. For more information, see: http://mysite.freeserve.com/DebjaniChatterjee

The Yeti Hunter

Debjani Chatterjee

*T*hroughout history Europeans have viewed India as a
land of spices, precious stones, indigo dye, silks and
other textiles, and have been eager to trade. In 1600 Queen
Elizabeth I granted the East India Company a charter that
gave it a monopoly of trade with India, and in 1612 the
Mughal Emperor Jehangir gave his permission for the Company to trade with India. Robert Clive (1725–74) was one of
many British adventurers who went to India to seek their for-
tunes. Clive and many others ruthlessly amassed so much
wealth that when they returned home to Britain they were
called 'nabobs' after the Indian title of 'nawab' for a ruler.

From being simply a trading company the East India Company gradually assumed political control in parts of India. Its
policy of 'divide and rule' played off one Indian state against
another until by the 1850s most of the country came under
British rule. Many in Britain came to believe that their
'success' in India and in other parts of Asia and Africa was
evidence of their racial and cultural superiority. They
believed that they had a mission to bring 'civilization' and

Christianity to other peoples. Indians revolted in 1857, an uprising long described by British historians as the 'Indian Mutiny' and by Indians as the 'First War of Indian Independence'. The Indian subcontinent finally gained its independence in 1947, but millions of lives were lost in the struggle and during the partition of British India into India and Pakistan.

For many westerners, the Himalayas have always been symbolic of all that they consider remote and mysterious in the East. Everest, the highest mountain in the world, is a sacred mountain for the Tibetans and the Sherpas, which they call Chomolungma. Westerners named it Everest after Sir George Everest, a British surveyor-general of India. After the North and South Poles had been reached in 1909 and 1911, Everest was called the 'third Pole' and various European countries mounted expeditions to 'conquer' it, ignoring the fact that the Sherpas have always lived there and climbed its rugged terrain as a matter of routine. These expeditions failed until in 1953 the British Everest Expedition set off to climb the mountain. New Zealander Edmund Hillary and his Nepali Sherpa guide, Tenzing Norgay, were the only expedition members to reach the summit. Hillary was knighted by Queen Elizabeth II and Tenzing received Britain's George Medal. The West has only recently begun to acknowledge the achievements of Sherpa mountaineers.

For centuries the Himalayas have been associated with stories of a fabled being called the 'yeti'.

'This is definitely it, Sandra, the big one!' Clive Adams almost screamed at his research supervisor. 'I feel it in my bones. This summer is all I ask for – just one more stab at the yeti. It's the jackpot this time, for sure. Jamling has told me of a recent reliable sighting on Kanchenjunga.'

The yeti! The Abominable Snowman! Sherpa Jamling Gampo had told Clive that the word was derived from *yah* meaning 'rock' and *teh* meaning 'animal', so the yeti was 'the rock-living beast'. How the very name echoed, for Clive, with the sound of eastern mystery and legend. For as long as he could remember Clive had been obsessed with the yeti. He had spent every penny that he had on geography magazines, the way other kids bought CDs and DVDs. It was in one of these magazines that he had first seen photographs of strange footprints in the snow. These old photographs, taken by the British mountaineers Eric Shipton and Michael Ward in 1951, showed footprints thirty to thirty-five centimetres long. The caption read: 'Could these be the footprints of the Abominable Snowman?'

Since then he had collected anything and everything that he could find on the subject, though admittedly more of his material was fiction than fact. There was the account, for instance, of Captain d'Auvergue, curator of the Victoria Memorial in Calcutta in the heyday of the British Raj. Snow-blinded, he had nearly died of exposure on the high Himalayas, but returned with a fascinating tale of meeting a yeti that was about three metres tall. Of course, not many had believed him.

So little was known about the yeti that it did not need a great deal of effort for Clive to pass himself off as something of an expert by the time he was a teenager. He would talk endlessly to anyone who would listen – about the

Himalayan yeti, the Californian Bigfoot, the British Columbian Sasquatch and all the other variations on a hairy and baffling giant humanoid rumoured to inhabit remote mountainous regions.

As the years passed and more and more sightings were reported and articles written, Clive's obsession grew. Others might see and measure footprints, find and analyse dung, even on rare occasions see an indistinct form that could be a yeti, but he, Clive, would be the intrepid hero who would not only explore the Himalayas – 'the abode of snow' – but also prove the creature's existence to the world. The yeti haunted his childhood and adolescent dreams.

And it was always the same dream: in a game of hide-and-seek in a desolate wilderness of endless mountain ranges he would hunt for the yeti. At times he would catch a tantalizing glimpse and give chase, but then at some point their positions would be reversed and he would be running and tumbling in a panic as the elusive creature closed in on *him*. The instant before his capture, Clive would wake up, bathed in a cold sweat.

His school counsellor had clearly fancied his single-parent mum and told her not to worry, that Clive would grow out of his obsession – 'It's typical of such brainy lads,' he said – and with it his nightmares. 'The yeti represents a father-fixation,' pronounced the amateur psychologist. 'Mrs Adams, your son both needs to find a father and at the same time fears what he may find. As he gets older he will grow in confidence and leave behind his youthful fantasies.'

The counsellor was so wrong! He had said that Clive's lack of friends was down to shyness over his pimply face, and that the lad would soon find a girlfriend and develop new interests. But Clive never did. And as for wishing for a father, he showed little curiosity in knowing about his dad. Mrs Adams consoled herself that Clive was just putting up a teenager's devil-may-care front. But the single-minded interest in the yeti remained and grew with the years.

Clive's meeting with Sherpa Jamling Gampo in Darjeeling had been a turning point in his life. He had never met anyone like Jamling before. Wiry and muscular, Jamling had a round brown face with expressive black eyes. He knew seven languages and appeared to speak English with ease, though his expressions were perhaps a little old-fashioned and he often let his strong hands and mobile eyebrows speak for him. A Nepali Sherpa graduate from the Tenzing Institute of Mountaineering, Jamling knew far more about the yeti than Clive, but he seemed to wear his knowledge lightly.

Breathlessly Clive had told him about his very first expedition in Nepal: 'I couldn't believe my luck. There it was – a large white figure in the snow. It *had* to be the yeti. It couldn't be anything else.' Jamling just laughed, as he often did at Clive's comments – something that Clive found quite maddening. 'What's so funny this time?' he demanded.

'Maybe it was the yeti,' said Jamling slowly, but then he shrugged his broad shoulders and laughed again – 'or maybe not.'

'What else could it be?' asked Clive. Damn the man! Polite though he was, Clive was often sure that the Sherpa was mocking him.

'Adam Sahib, in the snow eyes sometimes play tricks.'

Jamling always called him 'Adam Sahib'. Clive did not like the formality of what he was told was the Sherpa equivalent of 'Mr Adam' and had asked him to call him by his first name. But, 'No, Adam Sahib,' Jamling had said.

'Adam is a fine name for you. And all white men are sahibs, after all.'

'But Clive's a fine name too,' said Clive. 'I like to think of Lord Clive of India.' He considered his namesake from history books. The adventurer Robert Clive had been a young tearaway from Shropshire, a bit of a hooligan who had gone to India in the days of the East India Company and accumulated great fame and fortune.

'No, no, Adam Sahib, Clive was most definitely not "of India". He was a pukka sahib like you, a total foreigner. He was also a *badmaash*, a scoundrel who looted our country and left with his ill-gotten riches. You must not be like him.' Jamling shook his close-cropped head and seemed emphatic on this point. Then he smiled. 'But Adam was the first man in the Holy Bible and the Holy Koran, so—'

'Yes, yes, and *I'll* be the first man to find the yeti,' interrupted Clive excitedly.

Jamling laughed aloud, his bright eyes dancing. 'But, Adam Sahib, how can you be the first when we Sherpas have already encountered the yeti so many times over the years?' Then he added more kindly, 'Perhaps, though, you will be the first sahib.'

This soothed Clive somewhat. 'Really, Jamling? You know, I don't mind if I can't bring a live yeti back to civilization with me, but I'm absolutely determined to bring back physical evidence of the mysterious creature's existence: even a sample of blood or fur for DNA testing would be proof enough.'

Jamling merely raised his eyebrows: 'Who is to say what is civilization, Adam Sahib? Do you mean your world in the West? What about this ancient land?'

'Well, er . . . you know what I mean,' Clive stammered.

But he joined in Jamling's merry laughter when the Sherpa added, 'Perhaps the yeti too has a civilization? Have you considered it? Would the yeti think it civilized to hunt the yeti?'

Clive slapped the Nepali on his back. 'Jamling, you are such a tease!' he said. 'But you *will* help me to find it, won't you?'

Jamling shrugged. 'If it is to be.'

Clive was convinced that what he had seen in Nepal had been a yeti, but before he could get his camera ready it had vanished in the mountain mist. All he had managed to capture on his film was a tiny blurred outline that could be almost anything or anyone. Nothing in the picture gave a sense of proportion. It could have been an out-of-focus photograph taken in any snowy place – perhaps even one of the hilly areas in the Peak District around Sheffield where he lived. All he had was the snow scene and his diary entry to back up his claim that the picture came from an altitude of almost 5,000 metres in Nepal in high summer and not Sheffield in the middle of winter. But even the best photographs could lie, he consoled himself. How often had photographs of fairies, ghosts and Loch Ness monsters turned out to be hoaxes? Clearly, it needed more than photographs.

Clive joined a climbing club in Barnsley and took every opportunity to spend his vacations trekking and mountain climbing in Nepal and India. While his fellow members enjoyed climbing for its own sake, for Clive it was simply a means to an end. He was always questioning Jamling and his fellow Sherpas about the yeti. One of the other Sherpas had told him that Jamling's nickname for him was 'yeti hunter'. Clive had learned a lot from these mountain folk.

Now in his twenties, Clive maintained his own website on

the yeti and believed that he was an expert on the subject. Through the Internet he kept in touch with a small network of yeti scholars who shared his enthusiasm. He had no time for a social life. The pubs-and-clubs scene – so popular with other students in Sheffield – held no interest for him, so this select group of people on the Internet, his discussion group, were the closest he had to friends. But Clive also thought of them as rivals: too many of them were competing to be the first to make new discoveries about the yeti; some even hoped to find the yeti itself and tell the world about it. And the yeti was a subject about which Clive felt increasingly possessive. *He* alone had to be the first to discover it. He felt as if he was the leader of a hungry wolf-pack of yeti hunters, and there were one or two in the pack that were jostling to assert themselves. Soon they could be challenging his position.

Chief among his rivals was Li Chin from Sydney, a professional climber, photographer and trophy hunter. He seemed to have no problems in getting lucrative TV and publishing commissions that took him to the Himalayas. He had climbed many of the highest peaks, brought back several specimens of rare orchids and taken stunning photographs. Clive had admired his award-winning photographs of K2, Everest and Nanga Parbat, but at the same time he thought that Li Chin was wasting opportunities that he would die for. The yeti had so far eluded Li Chin, but Clive fretted that, with such support, the Australian could get there ahead of him. And recently it seemed everywhere that Clive turned, Li Chin was already there.

Clive now smiled his most winning smile at his PhD supervisor. Dr Sandra Hartley sighed and observed the youthful egghead who was her youngest research student. Clive was lean and fit from all the climbing that he did. His spectacled face looked intense and there was a fanatical gleam in his steel-grey eyes. He was certainly very knowledgeable about his subject – he knew far more than she did – and by now was quite familiar with the Himalayan terrain and conditions. Yet she had her doubts about Clive: she had heard several uncomplimentary reports about his high-handed and egotistical behaviour on the campus, where he treated almost everybody as his inferior. More worrying still, at times he tended to get carried away with pseudo-scientific ideas about race and evolution, and it concerned her that he applied these to the yeti. She thought his views and arrogant attitudes were a hangover from a colonial past, and would have expected someone of his generation to have abandoned such outdated and racist notions. Moreover, he had already spent over two years of precious research time and his scholarship would soon be exhausted. As yet he had little to show for it and didn't seem at all concerned.

'Look, Clive, I sympathize with your ambitions, but you have only six months left and, on the work you have done, I can't recommend an extension. Face it – there are no yetis. And if there ever were, they're as extinct as the sabre-toothed tiger, the mammoth and the dodo. It's time you let go of your yeti hunt and concentrated on salvaging what you can of your PhD. Your trips to Nepal and the Sherpa interviews you've done have given you a wealth of documentation on yeti myths and legends. Sherpa Jamling Gampo too has given you much material from the Tenzing Institute. So it's not all been a waste. Why not write up all those notes and shape out a thesis on Sherpa folklore? I think you have some original material there and, properly written up, it could earn you your PhD.'

'Damn the PhD!' muttered Clive under his breath. All that mattered was getting his scientific proof. The PhD was only an excuse to spend every waking moment of his time researching the only subject that meant anything to him. But he knew that there was nothing he could say that would make Sandra relent.

'Oh, OK, I'll sort out my material with a new focus on yeti folklore,' he offered at last. 'But I'd like to read some of the Tibetan archive material in the National Library in Kolkata.' He appeared to brighten and warm to this new idea. 'You know, I could even go up to Dharamshala and Bhutan! The Tibetan yeti folklore will enrich my interviews from Nepal. That would make a really interesting thesis, don't you think?'

'Quite!' was Sandra Hartley's dry response. She couldn't quite believe Clive. Surely it was still the yeti – not the Dalai Lama – that he was after, so why visit Dharamshala? Tibetan archives indeed! As for the National Library of Kolkata – splendid institution though it was – Dr Hartley shrewdly guessed that Kolkata's attraction was only as a staging post to the hill station of Darjeeling and the majestic mountain peak of Kanchenjunga. Still, it was up to Clive now – she had done what she could in tutorials. Besides, he had no money left to finance a last yeti-hunting trip – or had he? She looked thoughtfully at the strange young man who had quickly gathered up his papers from the table between them and was now rushing off without even saying goodbye. Clive was like that – not rude exactly, but he had no time for polite niceties.

Clive stood with Jamling at a bend on the mountain road and looked across the valley at the familiar but amazing sight of Kanchenjunga at dawn. He took deep breaths as if he had been starving of oxygen. The world seemed fresh, newborn. The sun spread a glow on the snowy slopes that was the most delicately marbled pink. Like a lotus, thought Clive. No, more like the luminous pink inside a conch shell or even the rosy tinge that colours the marble walls of the Taj Mahal at sunset. 'You know, Jamling, I can well understand why through the centuries yogis came to these mountains to meditate on their beauty and serenity. And even though you have Everest and other mountains in Nepal, I can understand how the Kanchenjunga would draw you.'

Jamling smiled and his eyes danced fire, but he said nothing. Clive shook his head as if to clear it of fanciful thoughts.

He had come to Darjeeling, his last stop for stocking up on food, medicines, maps, torch batteries, camera equipment, rope and whatever else Jamling advised him to purchase for his survival on the mountain. It was the logical place too for hiring his Sherpa guides, but this time Jamling was all Clive could afford. On previous expeditions he had been part of a team and there had been many Sherpas to carry their equipment and set up camps for them at appropriate altitudes. But now he did his best to persuade Jamling that they would climb Kanchenjunga by themselves.

'Where is your courage, Jamling, your sense of adventure?'

Jamling curled his lip and said, 'Adam Sahib, you have watched too many *Indiana Jones* movies. I saw one on TV – Indiana Jones is a sahib who always comes completely unprepared to jungles, mountains and caves, but he has the luck of fools and always escapes somehow *and* brings back the treasure.' Then he laughed as he added, 'People say that

Bollywood films are fanciful, but I think they're more true to life than your *Indiana Jones* movies.'

'But think how famous we'll both be after our yeti adventure,' pleaded Clive. 'You know that the West doesn't believe the yeti exists. Just think – we'll do what even Sir Edmund Hillary and Sherpa Tenzing Norgay couldn't. They saw the yeti's giant footprints in the snow on Everest, but they couldn't find the yeti, they couldn't bring back any evidence. *We* will.'

Jamling looked pityingly at the Englishman. 'Hillary Sahib climbed Everest, and when he came down from the top, he said, "We've knocked the bastard off!" Like you, he wanted the yeti. He saw footprints on Everest and became a yeti hunter. He returned to the mountain with a big expedition and spent much time and money. But he could not find the yeti. For Sherpa Tenzing, and for all of us Sherpas, Everest is always Chomolungma, "Mother Goddess of the Earth". He climbed Chomolungma to make her an offering and he taught many others to climb. He did not bother about the yeti. He knew that the yeti comes when it wants and to whom it wants.'

This made no impact on Clive. 'Look here, I'll carry my share of the gear,' he offered. 'We'll travel light and fast.'

Jamling looked grave. 'Adam Sahib, if there's no money for Sherpas, it's better that you don't go up Kanchenjunga.'

But Clive pleaded. 'OK, we'll only go part of the way. I just have to do it, Jamling, with or without you. I know that the yeti is my destiny. And I have enough to pay you.'

The Nepali raised his eyebrows, but at last agreed to accompany Clive on condition that they would turn back whenever Jamling said it was too dangerous to go on. This time they would carry only what was absolutely essential.

With high hopes, Clive joined Jamling in giving a final check of all their gear and, with a silent 'nothing ventured – nothing gained', he strode off into the forested slopes above the sunlit Darjeeling valley, closely followed by his Sherpa companion.

By midday Clive and Jamling had made good progress. The weather had remained glorious, but they knew from experience that it could change at any moment and become impossibly violent. Clive was breathing heavily and his limbs were tiring, but he felt mentally alert. Only a lone eagle had flown overhead all day, but he knew, with total certainty, that they were not alone – somewhere in the snowy wilderness ahead of him was the yeti, his Abominable Snowman. Clive could almost sense its presence and often found himself stopping and looking up at the mountain ahead, half expecting to see the yeti gazing down at him.

Once or twice Jamling gave him an odd look. 'Adam Sahib, are you OK?' he asked. But Clive, panting, just gave a thumbs-up sign that all was well.

In the late afternoon Jamling insisted they stop to drink their Thermos drinks, eat some meagre rations and listen to the radio before starting upwards again. There was concern in his bright eyes and Clive noticed that, along with the white glucose tablets, his companion had slipped him altitude-sickness pills.

'Yeh akaashvani Dilli hai,' announced a news presenter in Hindi.

'English, let's have English,' snapped Clive, impatiently searching for another channel.

Jamling frowned. 'We should listen to the weather report, whatever the language, and I will translate for you.'

Clive paid no attention.

'*A leading Himalayan explorer was interviewed today in Darjeeling. A world authority on Alpine and Arctic wildlife, Mr Li Chin is here to—*'

The rest of the radio speech was drowned in crackle. Clive gave a strangled cry and shook the radio in frustration. Swiftly Jamling reached across and turned it off.

The pills were never swallowed as a sudden flurry of snowfall on a slope some distance away caught Clive's attention. He reached for his binoculars. He didn't dare allow himself to hope; he had been disappointed too often in the past. Too many times an object in the snow had turned out to be nothing more than a snow hare, well-camouflaged against the white background, or a snow leopard bounding silently away.

Clive was momentarily frozen to the spot. Through his binoculars he could see a giant shape; it was furry like a polar bear, and standing upright on hind legs. The creature was gazing directly at him. White fur covered its entire body, even the face, and its bright shining eyes seemed to be measuring him. Clive shuddered and screamed with excitement: 'Look, Jamling! There it is! Look.' He thrust the binoculars into the Sherpa's hands; he so wanted to share the miracle he had just seen.

Jamling stood by his side and focused across the icy wilderness to where Clive was pointing, but his expression remained unchanged. Clive watched with impatience and frustration as his companion slowly took in the distant horizon, turning all around for a panoramic view. 'Did . . . did you see it?' he asked eagerly.

Jamling ignored the question. Instead he urged Clive, 'Adam Sahib, the weather is changing. Soon there will be danger for us. We must leave now.'

Clive looked at him in astonishment. 'We can't possibly leave now! The yeti's out there! Don't you understand? It's my big break!'

When Jamling pulled at Clive's arm, the Englishman let fly wildly with his fist and soon the two men were tumbling down the snow-covered slope.

Jamling was the first to stand up. Pulling Clive up, he frowned as he said, 'I can't force you, but I'm going back. We can't fight bad weather.'

'I'll not pay you if you go,' said Clive cunningly.

But Jamling repeated, 'We must leave *now*. Money isn't everything. You promised we would leave.'

'Never!' panted Clive. 'You go if you're afraid. I'm staying.' He grabbed back the binoculars, but to his dismay there was nothing to be seen now. 'Damn you, Jamling! It's gone and I can't waste any more time arguing with you.' And with that, he started towards the spot where he had seen the creature.

Jamling shook his head as he watched him go. Joining his palms together in a Nepali farewell to Clive's back, he said softly to himself, 'Find what you want, Adam Sahib. Kanchenjunga waits.' Then he turned away to retrace their path down the mountain.

It took Clive an exhausting hour of scrambling through the snow to reach the place where he was certain that he had seen the yeti. His adrenalin kept him going, but when he arrived there was no sign that anything had been there. Clive looked around, baffled. He tried to guess at the height and weight of what he had seen. Surely something over three metres tall and weighing at least 250 kilograms couldn't just disappear into thin air? But there weren't even any footprints. Jamling had not seemed to notice anything

– or had he only pretended to see nothing? Had it been a hallucination? It didn't bear thinking about after all this effort. Had he missed the right spot or gone past it? Had he even gone in the wrong direction? Clive suddenly panicked as the loss of his rucksack during the tussle with Jamling finally sank in. Bewildering doubts crowded in and agitated his mind.

He rested on his haunches and tried to calm himself. All the different yeti stories that Clive had ever heard from Sherpas exploded in his head: yetis were Tibetan lamas in a previous incarnation; yetis would only communicate with shamans with mystical powers; yetis couldn't have children and so kidnapped human babies; yetis lived twice as long as human beings; yetis could appear and disappear at will; it was bad luck to kill a yeti; a yeti's call was so high-pitched that only dogs and other yetis could hear it . . . 'All rubbish!' some people said, but Clive was convinced that there was more than a grain of truth in such tales and he intended to prove it.

Calmer now, he looked back at the lower slopes. His own footprints were all too visible, as was the long metre-wide groove created when he and Jamling had slid down the mountainside in their crazy fight. He looked at the spot where he judged the yeti had stood and saw that it was like a platform – you could stand or sit there and gain a panoramic view. He patted the ground with gloved hands. It was not so much snow as ice, packed solid and smooth, as though it had been frequently compressed. He felt he was getting somewhere at last, and shivered with cold and anticipation. This was obviously the yeti's territory, for who or what else would have pressed the snow into ice with its weight at this height above sea level?

Then it came to him – if this was the yeti's place, it might come back here. All he had to do was wait, though patience was not in his nature. He might have hours to kill. He didn't want to admit to himself that it might even be days or weeks, or that his theory might be wrong, of course, and that the yeti might never return. Besides, the feeling of the creature's proximity that had haunted Clive all the way up the mountain returned stronger than ever. Perhaps even now the yeti was watching him. He wanted to explore the mountain slopes around, but it was suddenly growing darker and the temperature was dropping rapidly. He had to find a place to shelter for the night. The platform was not wide enough, nor was it protected from the icy wind.

The slope above him was so steep that it was almost vertical, and the ice was so smooth that it reminded him of the glass mountain in a fairy tale. Didn't the prince have to scale the glass mountain to win his princess? Climbing alone as he was – and that in itself was foolish – Clive didn't dare attempt the slope. In fact he doubted that anyone could climb it. He looked back in the direction from which he had come. In the semi-darkness, that too looked dangerous, but he had no choice now. It was beginning to snow and soon his tracks would disappear. He had already stayed at the platform too long. Gingerly, he made his way down through the snow, picking away at the ice for toeholds. It took him what seemed an eternity to return to the place where they had stopped to drink: Clive his cocoa and Jamling his butter tea. At least he *thought* it was the same place, but he couldn't be sure.

Clive was in the grip of a ferocious snowstorm now. By disregarding the weather signs, he had neglected the most basic rule of mountain climbing. There was no point now in trying to find a more protected position. Clive rummaged in the snow to see if he could retrieve any of his belongings. Already he had lost his digital camera, binoculars, radio, emergency flares and most of his supplies. All he could find was one of Jamling's triangular red prayer-flags planted in the snow. Frustrated at the uselessness of finding a prayer-flag, Clive kicked at it with his boot and, as the snow flew, he discovered that his heavy-duty sleeping bag lay beneath it in a tight bundle. It seemed a godsend to Clive. So the Sherpa had not made off with *all* their belongings after all, he reflected. He felt a little ashamed that he had mentally branded him a thief. And he had to admit that Jamling had been right about the turn in the weather. But the knowledge did not make Clive feel any better. If he came out of this blizzard alive, he promised himself that he would leave the mountain and make his way back to England. All he could do for now was huddle inside his sleeping bag, trying to make himself as small as he could, grit his teeth and hope that the storm would soon pass.

What would Sandra say if she could see him now? He laughed to himself. Would he be able to send any of his website discussion group a last text message? But his mobile phone was lost in the snow. Li Chin's email, received just before Clive had left England, had suggested they do a 'joint investigative foray' in the Himalayas. Clive had not cared to reply. Well, why should he? 'Nothing doing, man,' he muttered now. He was feeling on the offensive; he would share his yeti with no one. Clive was annoyed to think that Li Chin too had come to Darjeeling, and wondered if the intrepid Australian, who had climbed several Himalayan peaks, knew this particular climb. But at any rate, Li Chin had not seen the yeti, while he, Clive, had done so – twice. He laughed again, and broke into a hacking cough.

Clive felt strangely light-headed. The harsh wind seemed to have detached his head from his body. He was a Himalayan eagle, and looked down below where his sleeping bag, with his body inside, was a tiny mound of snow. An igloo. 'Eskimos live in igloos made of solid ice,' his mother had told him in his childhood – how many years ago? 'Inuits, Mum, not Eskimos,' he muttered into his sleeping bag.

Rambling thoughts crowded into his head. No one in England knew that he was on Kanchenjunga, though he suspected that Sandra had not been fooled by his so easily agreeing to change the topic of his thesis. Now even Jamling had gone away and he was alone. 'All alone with the yeti,' he murmured to himself.

The snow became a giant arm and eagle-eyed Clive watched his sleeping bag being tossed in the storm. But he had no sensation of pain. If hypothermia didn't kill him first, he would certainly be crushed to death. Some part of his brain had detached itself from the scene. He remembered learning about the bone-crusher bird that threw down bones from a great height to smash and reduce them to more manageable bite-size pieces. So, was the giant going to eat him? He puzzled over whether the yeti was a bone-crusher. How big would its bite-size pieces be? 'So much material, Sandra, for my thesis,' he whispered in wonderment.

From time to time Clive opened his eyes, but it took a long time for the immense cave interior to come into focus. He lay perfectly still and took in the high-domed ceiling first. There were glittering stalactites of a size and beauty that made the cave seem like an immense cathedral in the snow. Who would have believed that this place existed inside the mountain? A slight sound made him turn his head. Just a few metres away a yeti sat cross-legged and stretched his powerful arms – no, *her* arms. From so near, Clive could make out the fur-covered breasts. He smiled and the yeti smiled back. The teeth looked gleaming white and not unlike his own. She was probably omnivorous.

'Thank you,' said Clive softly. 'You saved my life.' Clive had a moment's doubt as to whether she understood his speech. Did yetis have a language? But she nodded, and he was reassured.

The yeti shuffled across and put a large furry hand on his sleeping bag. Clive counted five digits. How human the creature looked! He knew the theory about the yeti being a missing link to humanity's first ancestor, but he had never given it much credence. The thought floated into his head that she might be the result of some parallel evolution, perhaps a species that acquired mutant genes very early in human history. He wondered now if there was some way in which he could clip a sample of that long white fur. Her lustrous green eyes were really quite lovely. What a tender maternal expression they held! He observed with interest that while one eye remained focused on him, the other had swivelled direction, just as a lizard's might do, to look beyond him. And the yeti's eyes also had a protective nictitating membrane – the inner eyelids that were distinctive of many reptiles and evidence, some said, of evolution from the sea. It was fascinating to watch her blink. 'No wonder you don't go snow-blind,' he commented. The yeti said nothing. Perhaps she could not talk.

There was no fire in the cave, but Clive noticed that it was not cold. If anything, he was feeling rather warm inside his polypropylene bag.

All of a sudden a faint noise invaded the sanctuary of this ice-sculptured cave. He wondered what it was, but his rescuer had heard it too and she frowned slightly. She placed a long white finger across her shapely lips to silence him. But Clive was bursting to know – to know everything.

'What is it? Another yeti?'

'No, another yeti hunter trying to climb the mountain.'

Clive was too astonished to reply. The yeti had spoken, but her lips had not moved. Ventriloquism? No, telepathy more likely. Could this primitive creature be a telepath? And how did she know that a 'yeti hunter' was out there on the mountain? He felt a momentary twinge of shame at his own nickname, given by Jamling. Did she not realize that he too was a 'yeti hunter'?

'Be quiet and stay still.' She spoke again with sealed lips. 'I will go and make sure that we are not in any danger.'

'But why?' Clive persisted as he quickly scrambled out of his sleeping bag and followed her to the cave entrance. If there was danger from the climber outside, surely it was the yeti who should take cover?

Clive stood beside her on the platform and looked down at the tiny figures below. There were four of them and, even at this great distance, he could see and hear them quite distinctly. From their clothes, three were clearly Sherpas carrying heavy loads on their backs. One of them was pointing up at him. Climbing ahead of them, and carrying a camera and a rifle, was a man whom Clive immediately recognized as someone he had felt happy to have beaten in the race to find the yeti. 'Li Chin!' he shouted, and waved his arms. The startled Australian looked up and then, to Clive's horror, raised his rifle.

'Don't shoot, she's harmless!' he shouted. But it was too late. The bullet missed the yeti, but grazed Clive's shoulder. Li Chin was now calmly pointing his camera to take a photograph. Didn't he know what he had done? 'You murdering idiot!' screamed Clive as he shook his fist in the air.

The next moment, he felt himself pushed back inside the cave and pinned down to the icy floor. The yeti's furry chest tickled his own and she had her huge hand clamped over his mouth to shut him up. 'This is the only place we can be totally safe,' she said. 'They will not be able to climb the ice field.'

The poor creature did not understand that it was now Clive's turn to protect her! 'It's OK, stay cool,' he said soothingly. 'He'll not hurt you once he recognizes me and learns how you saved me from the blizzard. I know the guy; he's a sort of friend and I'm sure he'll be satisfied with some long-range photographs.'

The green eyes looked liquid with a warm compassion. 'It is you who are new and don't understand,' she said. 'Yetis have no outsider-friends, only each other.'

Her large white hand was still clamped firmly over his mouth. Clive knew with a sense of delicious shock that he too had been communicating with his mind. All his senses were heightened, magnified many times. He looked down at the scratch left by the human's bullet in his massive snowy shoulder. His shaggy white feet were enormous, larger than any footprints he had seen in photographs. He looked back into her eyes and was not surprised by the reflection that he saw in them – a magnificent Abominable Snowman.

Jamila Gavin

Jamila Gavin's Indian father and English mother met as teachers in Iran. Jamila was born in the foothills of the Himalayas in India, but before the age of eleven she had lived in an Indian palace in the Punjab, a flat in a bombed-out street in Shepherd's Bush, a bungalow in Pune, near Mumbai, and a terraced house in Ealing. She now lives in a little town cottage in Stroud, Gloucestershire.

As well as living in lots of different places, she also went to lots of different schools and had many different friends. But two things stayed the same: her love of music and her love of books. As soon as she could read and write, she enjoyed making up stories, poems and plays, as well as composing music. Though she trained as a musician, it is through writing that she really feels she has been able to be most creative.

Jamila's *Coram Boy* won the 2000 Whitbread Children's Book Award, and her latest novel is called *The Blood Stone*.

Stab the Cherry

Jamila Gavin

Perhaps he fell in love with the drum before he was even born, lying there all tucked up in his mother's womb, listening to the *boom boom boom* of her heartbeat. And when he made it out into the big wide world, all he heard was the beat: the rhythm of life.

The deep vibrating bass line, accompanied by the powdery flurries of the drum machine, always stopped him in his tracks – sometimes mid-yell, his mouth wide open; or when the drumsticks burst into a rock fall of sound, like pebbles hurtling down a canyon – cascading into a space of sound. Soon as he could, he was rattling away with his fingers on the backs of biscuit tins, or picking up cutlery for drumsticks, driving everyone crazy.

Then Mr Robinson moved on to the estate and Dilip began to hear this amazing music coming out of his open window: guitars that seemed to scorch his skin, saxophones and trumpets flowing like liquid gold, and most of all the drums – rippling, thudding, hissing, heart-pounding drums. It blew his mind.

Some people thought it was strange for an old man to like that kind of heavy-metal music and super-funk, but Dilip just thought Mr Robinson was God. He felt as though he had connected with some kind of primordial past; that somehow Mr Robinson had been with him all his life, even before he was born.

They met when Mr Robinson almost fell over the boy, sitting on his doorstep, playing invisible drums on his knees in time to the *boom boom boom* pounding out of the living room.

'You like this kinda thing?' he asked in his deep fuggy voice.

'I want to be a drummer when I grow up,' Dilip had replied.

'You got a drum kit?'

'Nope.'

'You wanna try mine?'

Dilip's 'YES' was like the 'yes' of scoring a goal for England.

And that was the start of a beautiful friendship. Mr Robinson reckoned he could teach him a thing or two.

Mr Robinson had once been a professional drummer; he'd played with the best. But then he'd let things go – he was the first to admit it. 'I drank too much, smoked too much, experimented with this and that, got my priorities all wrong – and look what happened? Went down the bloomin' tubes.' He would sigh and show Dilip lots of photographs and press cuttings of him in his heyday, to prove what he once had been: touring America, being in the top ten, having the kind of money most people only dreamed of.

And then he lost it all. Lost control, lost his family, lost his money, lost his life. 'I lost everything. I wasted the best years of my life, man! Had to go busking to make enough money to live, but couldn't stop drinking and smoking rubbish. Landed up in the gutter,' he said. 'Slept rough, got so ill I nearly died – and who'd have cared? But then they gave me this flat and, somehow, I got my act together. Too late for playing any more. Too late.' He stretched out his old, black, gnarled, deformed hands. 'I'll never play again. Got arthritis now. Oh well – you'd better play *for* me.'

And so he'd begun to teach Dilip how to play drums – really play.

Not just *umpa umpa* – but the real complicated, syncopated thing.

And that's all Dilip ever wanted to do.

Then the Thuggis came into his life.

'Dilip! Where've you been?' his mother wailed as he walked in through the door and dumped down his school bag.

'Nowhere,' answered Dilip wearily. 'I ain't been nowhere – except school.'

'How come you're back so laaaate?'

Her voice irritated him. She'd done nothing but get at him lately.

'I'm not laaaate,' he mimicked cruelly.

'Hey you! Don't you be rude to Ma.'

Dilip hadn't noticed his older brother Mukham sitting in the living room in front of the ever-flickering television screen. He leaped over the back of the sofa holding up a reproving hand. 'If Mum asks where've you been, you answer politely. Gettit?'

'It's all right, son. Don't get angry. He didn't mean it.' Their mother grasped Mukham's threatening hand and pushed it down out of harm's way. 'He's done nothing wrong. He's a good boy, aren't you, Dilip?' She pinched his cheek. He pulled away as if to avoid an annoying fly. 'It's just that I worry – you know, with so many bad things happening out there.' Her voice rose again helplessly.

'Yeah . . . well . . . that doesn't mean he can be rude to you. Gettit, brother?'

Dilip snorted, 'Gottit', and pounded upstairs to his room.

He shut his door without slamming it, but his whole body was seething with fury and confusion. He went to the window and looked out. They were still there, the Thuggi Gang, lounging beneath the cherry tree. One of them was digging a knife into its bark.

Downstairs, he heard the front door open then close, and he saw Mukham crossing the green patch of grass to join them.

That's what made Dilip feel so angry. If anyone was bad in his family it was his older brothers Arjun and Mukham. They were both members of the Thuggis, and had been ever since they went to secondary school, creating mayhem round the neighbourhood and terrorizing anyone that stood in their way.

Now Arjun was in prison for stealing cars, a habit he'd picked up on the estate with the gang, and Mukham already had a reputation, worse than Arjun. He walked with a limp, which he was proud of because his knee had got smashed in a pitched battle with the Trouts – the white boys' gang whose territory was down the hill on the Troutwater Estate. He claimed that no one could get the better of him, even if he'd broken both legs; even if he'd been in a wheelchair.

Mukham must have known why Dilip was late home. It

was because the Thuggis were out to get Dilip to join them. Almost every Asian kid like himself was expected to, once they got to Bayford Manor.

Life had been good up until then. He and his mates from junior school had all moved up to secondary together and he had continued to hang out with them – especially with his best mate, Russell. They were into their third year at Bayford Manor, and Dilip hoped he'd got away with it. But one day, he was approached by one of the gang. 'Ravi wants you in.'

Dilip had told Mukham, 'Please, Mukham, don't make me. Tell them I can't. I don't want to get into that kind of thing. It's not my scene, man.'

'Not your scene, man!' Mukhum had jeered. 'What is your scene, little brother?'

'Music. That's my scene, and there are white kids who are my friends and live on the Troutwater Estate. I'll never be able to go there if I join the Thuggis. Anyway, look what happened to Arjun. I don't want to get into that kind of trouble,' pleaded Dilip.

Muhkam had exploded with fury. He grabbed Dilip by the ear and twisted it till he stood on tiptoe with pain. 'You telling me you're a coward? You've got to grow up, mate. You've got to learn who your real friends are, and believe me – it's not that white trash down at Troutwater.'

He meant Russell. Mukham knew that Russell Bateman was his best friend. They both loved the same things: football, skateboarding, PlayStations – now it was music. They had already formed a group. Dilip had learned to play the bass guitar because they needed a bass player and he wasn't bad. But not as good as Russell, who was a brilliant guitar player – always playing along with Eric Clapton or Keith

Richards. Damien played the saxophone – he was good too – then Terry played keyboard and Wesley played drums.

Dilip had only wanted to play drums, but to begin with he hadn't got a drum kit of his own – and anyway, Wesley was their drummer and there had been no sign of him wanting to do anything else. Then, to his amazement, two things happened to change his life: Wesley of the drums suddenly fancied being a vocalist, and Dad, who had never seemed very interested in what he did, had bought Dilip a drum kit for his birthday. 'I must be some kind of masochist,' Dad had said ruefully. 'Mind you don't get us driven out of the neighbourhood with your noise.' But it was as if God was listening and didn't mind a bit. Dilip was ecstatic, and his dad almost joined the rank of God, along with Mr Robinson. Almost.

For a while, the gang didn't confront him again, so Dilip thought maybe his brother had said something. He was relieved. Perhaps Mukham was still his pal after all – just like in the good old days, when they had such a great time together and Dilip had hero-worshipped him. But Mukham had changed ever since he'd joined the gang. Everything had changed.

Dilip peered out of the window and prayed that Russell wouldn't come while they were still around. Mukham was talking animatedly to the group; he lit up a cigarette. They circled the cherry tree, kicked it and stabbed at it.

For the first time, Dilip noticed the tree. It had been outside his window ever since they moved there. Sometimes his mother sighed sentimentally that the tree had been planted the day they arrived. As far as Dilip was concerned, a tree was just a tree. But today, as he watched the lads attack its slender trunk, it felt like they were attacking him. He felt every stab and kick and stubbing out of the cigarettes. He wondered how long the little tree could bear the abuse. It looked vulnerable, all wintry and bare. It would surely die like all the other trees that the council had planted and the gang had vandalized.

Old Mr Robinson came walking by, slowly and stiffly, with a plastic shopping bag in his hand. He saw Dilip looking out of the window and gave him a friendly wave. The leader of the gang, Ravi Shah, turned and stared up at Dilip's bedroom window. Dilip ducked out of sight. His stomach fluttered with anxiety.

Ravi and his gang ruled the school playground and the whole estate around. The worst thing that could happen to anyone was to become their enemy, and to refuse to do something when they asked was unheard of.

The front door slammed. He knew it was Mukham. He heard his uneven step on the stairs, and then Dilip's bedroom door was flung open.

'Why don't you knock?' demanded Dilip.

'Shuttup,' retorted his brother. 'You're too cocky by half. They want you down there, Ravi and the others. Do you good to join the Thuggis. It'll soon clear the cockiness out of you.'

'Please, Mukham. Tell them I can't. Tell them I'm busy. I really don't want to join.' Dilip stopped trying to show his brother that he could stand up to him. He was begging him now; pleading with him.

'You've got to.' Mukham's voice was harsh. 'You'd better cooperate otherwise they'll get you, you cowardly little rat. You're letting the family down. Ravi won't be put off any more.'

'Russell's calling round in a minute. We're practising for

the gig next week and I may play drums. Please, Mukham. Tell them I'm ill. Tell them anything. After the gig, I'll do what you say.'

Mukham's eyes narrowed and he looked at him so hard Dilip thought he would strike him. 'Arjun would knock your head off for this. You know that, don't you? You'd damn well better be in with us by the time he comes out of prison.' Then he went to the window, opened it wide and leaned out. 'Hey, guys! Dilip can't make it tonight. Me mum's grounded him. Next time, OK?'

Ravi looked angry and kicked the cherry tree, shaking its early spring leaves.

The tree seemed to shudder with pain. Dilip shuddered with it. 'Thanks, Mukki. You're a pal.'

'Shuttup,' snorted Mukham, and slammed out of the room.

Nervously, Dilip watched his brother go and join his gang mates. He climbed on the back of Ravi's motorbike and, with a loud revving and yelling, stormed away.

Mum would have whined about that too, but she knew it was no use. Mukham was already a law unto himself. Their father worked all hours and was just too exhausted to be bothered. So long as the house was clean, tidy and peaceful when he came home, he didn't want to know. For him, it was eat supper, on with the telly, and bed.

Dad wasn't home yet, so it was OK to practise, but Dilip hoped Russell would come soon. He stared at his new drum kit. He was still awe-struck that he had his very own. Russell had wondered whether Dilip could take over from Wesley at the gig next Saturday. He was coming round to see if he was any good.

Dilip felt he was on the road to his destiny. Or was he?

Standing guard by the window, he saw Russell rounding the bend of the road with his guitar slung over his shoulder. The neighbourhood was quiet. There was no sign of the gang. Dilip quickly ran downstairs and opened the door to him.

The boys went up to Dilip's room, which these days looked more like a recording studio, what with speakers and cables and all kinds of gear he'd managed to collect. 'Right, Dilly, let's hear you then,' said Russell.

Excited but a little apprehensive, Dilip sat on his stool, his drum kit before him, and twirled his sticks.

As they ran through the numbers for their gig, Dilip forgot his anxieties, forgot himself. He was in seventh heaven putting into practice everything Mr Robinson had taught him: all those rhythms and rolls; when to clash the cymbals and when to pedal the pitch of the drums.

Russell was amazed and excited. 'Hey, you're really super-funky, man. Better than Wesley. We'll be a hit. Whaddya think? We'll really wow them next Saturday.'

'Yes, we'll wow them!' echoed Dilip, but he had to force an enthusiastic smile. He remembered the Thuggis and their threats. In the pit of his stomach, he was afraid.

Russell got up and put his guitar away. 'Better get back. We done good tonight, eh?'

Dilip accompanied him downstairs and opened the door. He would have slammed it shut again, but it was too late. They stood exposed in the outside light, visible to the gang, who had returned, silent as night birds, and stood waiting for them under the cherry tree. There was no running away.

'Good liar, your brother, eh?' Ravi stepped out of the shadows. 'Grounded were you?' he jeered at Dilip. 'More like you was *cohorting* with this white scum. Don't you know the rules of the gang? When I say come, you come.'

'I ain't part of the gang, so your rules don't apply to me,' retorted Dilip.

'Why you little . . .' Ravi ran forward and grabbed Dilip in an armlock, pulling his arm round his back.

'Leave him alone!' yelled Russell, rushing forward to help.

Another gang member stuck out a foot and tripped him up and Russell went crashing, guitar and all. The Thuggi put a foot on his chest as if he were a game hunter. 'What did you say?' he hissed, pressing his foot with each syllable.

'Mukham, tell them to leave him alone. He's my friend,' yelled Dilip, straining to escape from Ravi's hold.

'I'll deal with him,' said Mukham. He dragged Russell to his feet and scooped up the guitar.

'Dilly! What are they doing to you? Are you OK?' Russell struggled to see what was happening to his friend.

'He's just fine,' hissed Mukham in his ear, 'and if you want to stay in one piece, get the hell out of here and don't come back, see? Next time you may not get away so easily. Now scram.' And he pushed the boy into the road.

Before he turned the corner to leave the estate, Russell looked back. They had Dilip up against the cherry tree. 'Oh hell,' he moaned helplessly to himself. 'Hell, hell, hell, hell.'

Dilip felt the hard trunk of the cherry tree up against his spine. It seemed to whisper to him through his vertebrae. He looked up into the webbing of its spindly branches. Clusters of tiny buds, like pearls, were sprouting out of the wood. Ravi grabbed him by the chin and pulled his head level. 'It's no good. You're one of us, you know. The sooner you get that through your little pea-brain, the better. You spoil him, Muk,' he called over his shoulder to Mukham, who had rejoined the group. 'Tut-tut, Mukki-Mukki, you're supposed to be on our side. Keep this brother of yours in order next time.'

'Sure thing, Ravi!' Mukham answered. 'He'll stay in line, I promise.'

'He'd better,' Ravi sang threateningly. 'You're one of us now, you know, Dilip, and to prove it, we have a little task for you.'

What they asked of him made Dilip feel sick. It wasn't anything like running across the rails in front of a train, or stealing a car, or putting a brick through a shop window. He'd rather have done any of those things than what they demanded.

'That old geezer you're friendly with, 'im over there.' Ravi jerked his head in the direction of Mr Robinson's flat. 'He's got money stashed away – everyone knows that. He'll have got his pension today. I'm a bit short of cash at the moment, so I want you to get it.'

'I can't do that! He's my friend.'

'You'll do what we say.' Ravi looked threatening.

'No! No I won't!' blurted Dilip. 'You can't make me do that.'

'Oh, can't I?' Ravi came right up to the younger boy, eyeball to eyeball. 'Want to try me?' he asked, softly threatening. 'Can we make him do it, Mukki?'

'He'll do it,' reassured Mukham. 'I'll make flippin' sure he does.'

'Right then. Get that money. We'll be here waiting for you this time tomorrow. Have it, or else . . . Gottit?'

'Gottit,' muttered Dilip weakly.

Mr Robinson was looking tired when he opened the door to Dilip. 'Good to see you, mate!' he sighed, welcoming him in.

Dilip felt out of his body. That couldn't be him greeting his friend, coming as a thief and a traitor to betray him – could it? But it was him noticing how slowly Mr Robinson was walking, and that he winced when he moved. 'You OK?'

'It's been bad today. Goodness knows why. They can put a man on the moon, or clone a sheep, but they can't get rid of me blooming arthritis. It's this ruddy cold. Gets right into your bones. Perhaps I should go back to Jamaica.' He rubbed his knuckles. 'How's the drumming?'

'Great,' answered Dilip in a dead voice. 'Really great. I guess I shouldn't come bothering you day in day out. Now that me dad bought me that drum kit for my birthday, I don't need to play yours any more.'

'Hey, man, you never was a bother to me.' Mr Robinson's face broke into a smile. 'I like your company, and now you've got your own kit you can practise everything I teach you – and I've still lots more to teach you. Do you want to have a go now?'

'Yeh,' said Dilip, his eyes straying to the mantelpiece. He could see Mr Robinson's pension money tucked as usual behind the clock.

Dilip's voice was so unenthusiastic that Mr Robinson glanced quickly at him with concern. 'No one's making you if you don't feel like it.'

Dilip stood rock-still, his eyes still glued to the money, but in his mind's eye he saw himself standing under the cherry tree – waiting like the tree for the gang to come and kick and bully him. But he wasn't a tree, rooted to the ground, unable to fight back. Was he going to give in? He felt a rush of courage. Turning with a broad smile, he said, 'Yeh, please, Mr Robinson. I'd like a bash. We have a gig on Saturday at the Community Centre. It'll be my first big one.'

While Mr Robinson laid out the drum kit, Dilip could easily have plucked the money from behind the clock and pocketed it. But he had already made up his mind.

He stayed an hour and, with almost a sense of relief at having made his decision, bashed away all loose-wristed and free.

'Good, good!' applauded Mr Robinson.

They went through rhythm beats 4/4, 6/4 then 5/4, and practised twos against threes. 'Have a cup of tea . . . Have a cup of tea . . .' chanted Mr Robinson. 'That's the rhythm. Like rubbing your head and patting your tummy.'

The difficulties made Dilip laugh. His drum rolls rippled like hailstones, and when he hissed the brushes it was like soft rain. He almost forgot his troubles. He got the feel of the skin, letting the strokes rip then holding back to a soft *shoo . . . shoo . . .*

'Keep it dark, keep it nervous,' declaimed Mr Robinson. *Boom de-ka . . . boom boom de-ka de-ka . . . boom de-ka . . . boom boom de-ka de-ka . . .* 'Hear the syncopation interrupting the heartbeat.' *Paradiddle-diddle, boom ka boom ka boom.*

By the end of it, Dilip saw that Mr Robinson was sitting upright in his armchair, with closed eyes. His glance strayed to the mantelpiece and back again. He cleared his throat. The old man's eyes flew open. 'I'm off now. See you soon.'

'OK, OK, let yourself out, mate.'

'Did you get the money?' Mukham asked in a tense whisper, when he got home.

'Nope. I couldn't, Mukki. He's my friend.'

'You couldn't? You didn't?' Mukham was aghast. 'What do you think you're playing at? Don't you realize what they can do to you? What they could do to us? Do you want burning rags through the door?'

'I don't want to join the gang. Just leave me to my drums.'

'You and your blinking drums.' His voice rose from a whisper to a scream. 'You'll flipping well do as they say.' And, like a mad thing, Mukham was flinging open the window. He rushed round, yanking out the leads, picking up drums and sticks and cables and speakers and, before an appalled Dilip could comprehend what was happening, hurled them crashing out of the window to be smashed on the ground below.

'Mukki! For God's sake man, what have you done?'

Mukham turned a stricken face to him. Tears streamed from his eyes. 'Get real, man. Get real before they do something terrible to you.' Then he fled from the room and out of the house.

How terrible the world was. Dilip felt as though his life had ended. He stood at the window, staring out at the wreckage of his drum kit. People opened doors and peered out quickly, then shut them again and drew their curtains. A dog barked furiously, then was muffled. Downstairs, his mother was wailing with despair.

Like a sleepwalker, Dilip went out of the house. He walked across to the cherry tree and, leaning his back against its shining ringed trunk, slid down to its base.

Mr Robinson shuffled out painfully and viewed smashed drums and the bent cymbals. 'Why?' he asked, shaking his head in despair. 'Why would anyone do this?' He came and sat under the cherry tree next to Dilip.

The next morning, he didn't want to get out of bed.

'Dilip?' His mother came in anxiously and pulled the

curtains. 'You'll be late for school, darling. Won't you get up?'

Just when Dilip had thought his life was beginning, he felt it had ended. 'I'm sick, Mum, sick. I've got a headache. I'm not going to school.'

For a while, she sat on his bed and rocked silently, her body full of misery. 'I'm sorry, son, it's a real bad world. I'd take us all away if I could. Your father would too. But we can't. We're stuck here and have to make the best of it.' She stroked his head. This time, he didn't try to shake her off. 'We'll make Mukham pay for another drum kit. Your father will see to it.'

'Don't bother.' Dilip's voice was muffled through stifling his tears in the pillow. 'There's no point now. They'll never let me play with my group. Please just leave me alone.'

Later, the sight of the sun streaming into his room lured him out of bed. Listlessly, he went to the window and looked out.

He couldn't believe it. He gaped with amazement. The cherry tree had blossomed – just like that. It was a miracle. He couldn't think of the right words: it was like snow; like a fluffy white cloud had dropped into the branches; like a bride all veiled in white . . . like a warrior angel. Yes, that was it – that's what he was thinking: it was a warrior in shining armour. The bravery of the little tree – after all that kicking and slashing, to go and flower like that in the face of such ugliness. It was magnificent; it was a triumph. Now he knew: if that little tree had the courage to go and do its own thing, well, so could he. He got dressed with fast fumbling fingers, and raced round to Mr Robinson.

'Mr Robinson, I want to play at the gig on Saturday night. Thing is . . .'

'You'll need my drum kit,' smiled the old man. But his smile was sad. 'This is the worst thing that's happened since I moved here. But are you sure you want to go through with it? I know what they can do, these thugs . . .'

'Oh, I didn't think. They could smash up your drum kit too.' Dilip backed away, ready to leave in defeat.

'That's not it, lad. It's not my drum kit I'm worried about. It's you – and your family.'

'It's all right, Mr Robinson. I've made up my mind. I want to play – if you'll let me borrow your drums. I don't want them to win.'

'Right. You're on!' beamed Mr Robinson, and they shook hands on it.

The hall was packed that Saturday night. Sitting up there on the stage under the spotlight, Dilip had never felt happier. Everyone was playing like they'd been set on fire; they were inspired. Russell's fingers flew over the strings, and Wesley could sing, man – oh, yes, he could sing – his voice got everyone in the hall clapping and cheering. This made the rest of them play better than they had ever played before – and the cheers got louder and louder. Dilip's solo on drums was just coming up, when the doors at the back flew open.

There stood the Thuggi gang. They looked terrifying. Their faces were masked, they wore hooded bomber jackets and they carried baseball bats in their hands. The band straggled to a stop and the players looked round, bewildered. People were leaving fast, row on row. They didn't want trouble.

The gang began a threatening, slow, swinging march down the aisle. Mukham was among them. Dilip knew him by his limp.

'Oi, you! Dilip!' Ravi stopped and swung his baseball bat round and round. 'What the heck are you doing up there with the Trouts? Get on down here. You're leaving with us.'

Dilip sat frozen to his seat.

'Dilip!' It was Mukham. 'Don't trust your luck. Get on down here. What the hell do you think you're doing playing with this scummy lot?'

Still Dilip didn't move. He saw old Mr Robinson staring at him questioningly. Dilip thought of the brave little cherry tree, all showery flowery with blossom. *Don't give in, don't give in.* With a great yell, he struck his cymbals – and went off into an incredible riff: *bang, crash, swish, boom de-ka boom de-ka, pouf, paradiddle, hissss.* His sticks flew so fast they looked like twelve as they whirled through the air. People who were leaving stopped dead in their tracks. They turned to listen, then began cheering and clapping.

Ravi became enraged. Like a rogue elephant, he charged up on to the stage with his baseball bat swinging. He was about to bring it down on Mr Robinson's drums, when Dilip stood up in surrender and threw down his sticks. 'No, no! Don't smash them up. I'll come with you.'

'Oh no, you won't!' bellowed a voice from the back.

Everything stopped. The baseball bat hung in the air.

'Arjun?' Dilip couldn't believe it. His oldest brother, Arjun, who was supposed to be in prison, had been freed and was striding down the aisle.

'You leave my brother alone.'

Ravi leaped down and charged towards him. People scattered out of the way. He raised the baseball bat to attack, but Arjun grabbed his arm and, with a judo twist, landed the leader of the Thuggis flat on his back.

'Did you hear me?' asked Arjun, bending down over him.

'Don't you ever let me catch you bullying my brother again. And get this straight: he's not joining your gang. He's not joining any gang. He's not landing up in prison like me. Now get out of here, and take that lot with you,' he said, looking at the other gang members, who suddenly looked like nothing but a bunch of sheepish boys.

Mukham stood on his own. His mask had slipped from his face. He looked distraught, riven with indecision: whether to go with the gang or stay with his brothers.

'Mukham, whose side are you on?' Arjun touched his arm.

'Yours,' said Mukham. 'Yours, man.'

Later, when the gig was over, and the cheers and applause had filtered away into the night, Mr Robinson drove them home. The brothers unloaded the drum kit and were about to carry it into the old man's flat when he said, 'No, lads. Take it up to Dilip's room.'

'But, Mr Robinson . . . you can't . . .'

'Yes, I can. I want you to have my drum kit. It's yours, Dilip. If I'd had a son, I would have wanted him to be like you.'

'But how can I pay . . . ?'

'You damned well play as good as I once did, that's how.'

There was a shiver of wind. Dilip glanced at the cherry tree. Its blossoms were shimmering like moonbeams.

'If you can do it, so can I,' he whispered.

The cherry seemed to smile. Like a pattering, scattering, fluttering flurry of drumbeats, a shower of petals sprinkled to earth.

Adam Zameenzad

Adam Zameenzad was born in Pakistan and spent his early childhood in Nairobi. He went to university in Lahore, Pakistan, becoming a lecturer there, and later came to live and work in the UK.

He has had six novels published: *The Thirteenth House* (winner of the David Higham Prize); *My Friend Matt and Hena the Whore*; *Love, Bones and Water*; *Cyrus Cyrus*; *Gorgeous White Female*; and, most recently, *Pepsi and Maria*, which is about the lives of street children. His novels have been translated into many languages.

In his writings he tends to portray the lives of social outcasts, loners, losers, the deprived and the dispossessed. He aims to give voice to the voiceless, reshape and re-form those distorted by time and circumstance, embrace the rejects of this world, dignify 'trash' – white, tinted or tainted – and make visible the invisible. Adam takes a more light-hearted look at the outcasts at the centre of this story, which is part of a larger work.

Ali, the Elephant
and the Bicycle

Adam Zameenzad

Lost in the many layers of time and space lies the Kingdom of Nonsense, commonly known as *NoN*. Ali had just moved in there from VSL – a Very Sensible Land – and was finding it hard to adjust. People in *NoN* behaved very strangely, especially towards strangers, especially if they looked sensible. And Ali looked very sensible indeed! As did his mother. His father, however, had not been very sensible. Last year, in the Very Sensible Land, he refused to go to war with their neighbours, when it was evident to all sensible people that they should go to war with their neighbours. He was then taken by the *gaga* – Grade-A Government Agents. No one ever saw him again, nor knew what happened to him.

Later, the *gaga* came for Ali and his mother, Linta. Even though everybody assured them that mother and son were acutely sensible, the *gaga* would not believe them. Ali and Linta had to flee, along with many others, who were also wanted for not being sensible enough. After many months of travel, by boat and train and on lorries, they ended up in *NoN*.

Here they were to experience a totally new world, and different problems. The milkman would juggle three or four, even seventeen, milk bottles, dance with the cat, sing in a little girl's voice then disappear in a puff of smoke, sometimes forgetting to leave any milk behind – in which case the milk was delivered by telephone, which left a big mess on the telephone table, unless you were very careful.

Ali was a prone-to-fear boy, and today he was more than ever so prone – it being his first day at a *NoN* school. AND his thirteenth birthday!

He would be a teenager. And anyone sensible knew how dreadful teenagers were. Awkward, clumsy, unruly, ill-mannered, brutish, and totally, totally full of yuck and hormones – whatever *they* were! He would have given anything not to be thirteen, but he had nothing to give, nothing much – except a shiny green knapsack his very non-sensible grandmother had given him before she suddenly disappeared one breezy autumn day, with strict instructions not to use it before he was thirteen. He loved his grandmother, even the memory of her, and couldn't, wouldn't, give her last present away. Not that giving anything away could have averted the dreadful fate . . . the fate of being thirteen.

As for school: his school days at VSL had not been a rip-roaring success. Too stupid to hide his intelligence, he was harassed for being a smartypants; too weedy to fight back, he was hounded by the biggies. What would be in store for him here? The very thought sent him into throes of terror. Absolute, ultimate, mind-crunching, heart-pounding, gut-butchering terror. He was terrified of what the classroom would be like, what the wall posters would be like, what the dinner ladies would be like, what the toilets would be like . . . *And* he was terrified all the boys and girls here would look at him as if he were sensible. Which of course he was. Or so he believed.

But above all he was terrified of what the teachers would be like. This particular fear was multiplied by forever and a ten because of what a boy next door in the upside-down house told him about the teachers. *They take your work and fling it out the window until some bird brings it back in his beak, or throw it on the floor and jump up and down on it before chucking it in the bin.* When this made Ali really anxious, the boy said not to worry, for they always got their work back the next day, all neat and duly marked. And just as Ali began to look a little relaxed, the boy added, *You should watch out for the maths teacher. He likes to sit on your head, especially if you are new.*

It was a beautiful day. Warm, not a whiff of a breeze, still, silent – except for the odd cawing of a crow or a lark singing. With his curly brown hair all tidy, his new blue jacket and red tie – all bought from a catalogue on weekly payments – and his shiny green knapsack dangling from his back, Ali would have almost felt happy, had it not been for the test. When he had come to visit the school with his mother on the second Friday – they had two Fridays in *NoN*, because people liked Fridays, and no Mondays – the headmaster had told him he would have to take a test on his first day, Tuesday, which would have been Monday in VSL. It was on the basis of that test that the Head would decide which set to put Ali in.

Linta wanted to go in with him, just up to the secretary's

office, but Ali would not hear of it. He feared the others would think he was a mother's boy and make even more fun of him.

After embarrassing hugs and kisses from Linta and the promise of a wonderful surprise present for his birthday on his return home, Ali managed to free himself from her embrace and make for the school. He knew his mother was too poor, being a refugee from VSL, to buy him anything special, and it worried him that she might do something silly, like sell her wedding ring, to get him the bike he had always wanted. Not that he wouldn't have loved to have that bike. Lost in these thoughts, he had barely pushed open the main gate of the school when he flew upwards and hung suspended in mid-air.

It was a pleasant feeling. Pleasurable, even. Floating in the air like that. Like a bird. A bird sunbathing itself. Only there was no sun above him here. Even the sky had disappeared. Instead there was a cobweb-ridden roof that looked like it was going to collapse any minute. Below him was a lot of strange, gooey, messy stuff. Bunsen burners and test tubes and cylinders and bottles, scattered on the floor or sitting about on rows and rows of broken-down, tediously long tables. He must be dangling in some old, forgotten science laboratory.

'Thank the microwave you have come,' said a voice to Ali's right. 'I have been waiting for you since the year nineteen hundred and carbon dioxide. Ever since Ratty the pussy cat sprouted wings, carried me on her shoulders, flew up here, and dumped me without any explanation, or so much as a goodbye.' There was more than a hint of sour grumpiness in the voice of the speaker.

Ali turned his head to see who it was who had spoken. It

was an Indian elephant, quite inelegant, floating ungainly in the air, about a metre or so to his right. Ali could tell it was Indian and not African, by his ears, and the general size of him. And by his accent, of course. It was just like that of Mr Patel of the corner shop in his old country, though slightly different from Mr Patel of The Tandoori. But only ever so slightly different.

'Why were you waiting for me?' said Ali, quite spontaneously, forgetting his ever-present awkwardness over his high-pitched voice. What could the elephant have in mind? After all, he was a stranger. And everyone knew you had to be wary of strangers. Especially if they were elephants, and more so if they were floating elephants, *floating-in-the-air elephants,* Indian or African. From the local zoo, even. The neighbour boy had told him: *Beware of floating-in-the-air elephants, especially if they are strangers.* Or was it *strange*, or was it *passing strangers*, and not floating elephants at all? He couldn't be sure. He had been hanging about in this peculiar fashion for only a few minutes, if that, and was already beginning to lose sense of what was or was not said, and by whom. Perhaps it was his mother who had warned him against floating elephants. Floating-in-the-air elephants.

'And how did you know I was coming?' he continued, bringing his mind back to the present, putting aside his worries about who had said what and when and to whom, if at all.

'Here's how,' said the elephant, twisting his trunk round to get to the inside pocket of his grey jacket, pulling out a tiny piece of paper and handing, or trunking, it to Ali.

It was faintly printed, like a note from a Chinese fortune

cookie, only longer, like a long shopping list on a super-market receipt. It read as follows:

> *I'll tell you what you want to hear*
> *So wipe away that tear*
> *And jump down and up with joy*
> *Just wait for the boy*
> *Who'll save you from this dangling fate*
> *And put your feet upon the ground*
> *On a road that straight*
> *Leads you to the gate*
> *Of freedom for eternity*
> *But I tell you that it cannot be*
> *Not until a very sensible boy*
> *On his first day at silly school*
> *Falls sitting on a stool*
> *But without a stool*
> *Only then . . .*

Ali looked at himself. His bottom felt firmly settled, his thighs were projecting forward, his knees bent and feet dangling. Just as if he were sitting on a stool, the type of stool you have in some science labs at school. Only he wasn't sitting on a stool. Because there was no stool. But there might just as well have been one, for he was quite as comfortable as if he really were sitting on a stool!

'Hey,' shouted Ali, once he'd got over the surprise of his posture, 'most of it is torn off. It doesn't tell you what the boy is supposed to do.' For sure the paper was clumsily torn down the middle.

The elephant hung his head, as if in shame. 'I ate it,' he said in a low, hollow voice. 'Along with the cookie.' And when Ali gave him a dirty look and rolled his eyes to the sky – not that there was any sky here – the elephant changed his tune, or should it be tone, raised his head defiantly and said, 'You'd have done too! I was hungry. Just be thankful there's left what there's left. Imagine hanging in here with no grass or trees or any vegetarian cuisine since the year two thousand and helium!'

'You said it was nineteen hundred and carbon dioxide,' hissed Ali, outraged at the elephant's bad memory or outright lies or whatever it was. He wondered if he could ever again believe *anything* that outsize mammal had to say.

'You leave my mother out of it,' replied the elephant, nearly in tears.

'I never said anything about your mother!'

'Well then you *should* have! She was a good and kind parrot who gave all her wealth to charity and worked tirelessly for the United Nations.'

This wasn't taking them anywhere. Ali decided that since he was the superior mammal, it was for him to steer the conversation back to the matter in hand. Away from the practicalities of life, back to dreams. As his father used to say.

But he didn't want to sound dismissive of the elephant's mother. 'I do admire your mother tremendously for all her work. I'm sure she was the greatest parrot that ever lived. But for now, the point is, how does my being here help you?' he said. 'Now that the cookie poem has been swallowed by your huge mouthiness and is no longer here to guide us.'

'Oh *that*! That is *very* simple. You just sit on me. And the weight of the two of us together will take us both down. Then I can go out and eat my grass and bathe in the river and revel in the mud; and you can do . . . whatever ugly little boys like you like to do!'

'Thank you very much for that. As if I need reminding of my ugl— Forget it. You're no Mona Lisa yourself. And *where*, may I ask, is this grass and the river and the— Forget that as well. Let's get this getting-down job over with first. I am tired of sitting on this stool that is going nowhere – isn't even here.'

It turned out not to be quite as simple as that son of a parrot had implied.

It is not easy getting up on an elephant. In the best of conditions. Especially if you have not done it before. Halfway up in the air, without even a real stool to give you a lift up . . . No, it wasn't simple at all, no matter what the elephant said.

'It never used to be like this back home in India,' sighed the elephant after Ali had rolled over off his neck three times and hung on to his ears till they hurt. He was now in the throes of a passionate embrace with the elephant's left hind leg. Like they were Siamese twins instead of boy and elephant leg: left, hind.

'All the little boys, and big, used to climb up on my back with no trouble at all!' sighed the elephant all over again. And then again.

'I've had it,' said Ali as he fell out into the air yet another time. 'I am not going to make any more attempts to ride your fat back, just to help *you* out.' He was forgetting that it would be good for him, too, to be back on solid earth.

'Oh dear,' responded the elephant with weary resignation, 'I suppose we'll *have* to do it like it said in the cookie poem.'

So saying, he turned himself upside down, feet sticking up towards the ceiling.

'Try now.' He nodded to Ali, inasmuch as he could nod with his trunk pointing to the ceiling.

Ali tried, and this time was able to get on the elephant's back with no trouble at all. The elephant then turned over, and before Ali could scream, *Why in heaven's name did you not do this from the start, if you knew* . . . they hurtled downwards and fell with a resounding thud on the bottles and jars and things below. Foul-smelling liquids and potions of all sorts spurted out of the bottles until the whole floor was a pool of chemicals.

Some of the chemicals reacted with each other. A hissing sound, the smell of burning rubber, smoke, pongy gas . . . and within seconds both Ali and the elephant drifted into bleary-eyed unconsciousness.

As Ali's brain gradually rolled back into a semblance of normality, he heard a cheerily confident voice, at its most forceful, saying:

Sanitation, sanitation, sanitation.

It was the Head's voice! He had only heard it once before – but enough for it to be logged on his memory forever.

He forced himself to sit up, rested his back on the still-out-for-the-count elephant, rubbed his eyes with the back of his thumbs, and looked about him, tilting his head slightly upwards to see where he believed his Head's head might be. No sign of it.

I say to you, continued the Head's voice, *and I ask you to imagine. Imagine for a moment, if you please. Imagine that*

231

*the sanitation arrangements in this laboratory were perfect,
as indeed you and I would like everything to be. Yes, perfect!
Or even if they were adequate, merely adequate. Would then,
would then, I ask you most sincerely, would then these two
poor souls have been poisoned? Met their untimely death in
this cruel, heartless fashion?* Here the headmaster's voice
became slow and ponderous as he continued. *And we would
have been spared the tragic task of performing their funeral
rites. Especially on the ides of March. A lovely springy,
almost summery day. A time to be rejoicing in the birth of
new life, not mourning the deaths of this fine young man, and
that venerable visitor from India.*

'I am *not* dead,' cried Ali, as loud as he could, 'and
neither is elephant,' for Ali could hear the elephant's heartbeat as he sat leaning against him.

Ali, prone-to-fear Ali, was more frightened of being
buried alive than he was of dinner ladies. One of his recur-
rent nightmares had to do with live burial: of himself or his
mother or his father or anyone he loved; each time under
different and increasingly bizarre circumstances.

'Here. Look at me. I am alive. Can't you see me? I am
waving my arms about.' Ali's voice was becoming progres-
sively panic-stricken, hysterical even. 'Elephant is alive too,'
he screamed. For Ali had become rather fond of the
elephant, in spite of his stupidity, and was quite determined
to see the poor creature wasn't forced to his grave before his
time either. He'd have been better off hanging in the air
without Ali's help than pushed under a ton of dirt and rub-
ble with it. He should be well wary of following the advice
of Chinese fortune cookies in the future.

The Head seemed not to have heard him. *And now to
details of the ceremony*, he began again. *Dust to dust? Or*

*fire and ashes? What do you say? I shall arrange for a referen-
dum immediately. Pupil power is all-important to me. And I
shall do only as, and what, the pupils of this school want!
That is my unequivocal promise to my school, and to my
pupils! And to my countrymen, of course.*

Ali froze. He lost the strength even to shout any more.
Cremation! There was some hope in burial, but cremation!

Suddenly and mightily he realized he would rather be
thirteen than buried or cremated.

Fear sent his throat into hibernation, but his brain kept
functioning. Feverishly functioning.

The Head's voice must be coming through the school's
audio system. That's why he couldn't see the Head, nor
could the Head hear him. Someone – a nosy caretaker, or a
smelly dinner lady – must have come this way, seen him and
the elephant lying unconscious among the chemicals and
the fumes, presumed they were dead, and reported to the
Head.

All they had to do was to make themselves visible. Show
everybody they were not dead. And that was it.

'Get up, get up, you fat slob.' Ali shook, or tried to shake,
the elephant. 'Move, move before they bury us alive. Or
burn us. Get up. Get a move on!'

'Hey, boy . . . hold on, hold on . . .' The elephant finally
began to come round. 'What's the big hurry? I was just
going out for some curry . . . uh . . . oh . . .' he said in a
dreamy, half-awake sort of a way. Then, in a more alert
voice, 'Where am I? What's going on? What happened?
What's happening?'

Ali explained, as patiently as he could, considering the
state he was in. 'So, you see. We have to get out there. To

233

explain. Tell them we are alive, so they won't bury us alive, or worse, burn us down.'

'Why should we bother? Waste all that time and energy! Why not tell them when they come to bury us? After all, they cannot bury us, *or* burn us, not without getting to us first. And when they do, we'll tell them we're not dead. So there! Stop worrying, and go back to sleep.' So saying, the elephant was about to roll over and return to his sleep, but Ali was not going to let him off that easily. He couldn't fault the elephant's logic, though; but he still couldn't just sit there and wait. Just couldn't. He had to do something.

Besides, it wasn't as if they had been really sleeping. They were drugged. The fumes were still quite strong, and if they didn't get out of there, and soon, they might end up well and truly dead.

Holding his uniform tie between his teeth and up against his nose to ward off further fumes, he went over to the lab sink, filled a couple of tumblers with cold water, brought them round to where the elephant lay, and threw them over his eyes. The effect of this simple measure was astonishingly remarkable, taking Ali quite by surprise.

The elephant jumped to attention with the lightness of a kitten and, saluting sharply with his trunk, said, 'Private Joginder, sir. Reporting for duty, sir!'

Joginder must have been in the army at some point in his life. Of course it didn't take him long to realize where he was now, and with whom, but at least he was fully awake.

'Let's get out of here,' said Ali, taking command like a real lieutenant. 'You break through that door and I'll follow. We'll have a council of war beneath the trees at the back in 0.33 of a second.'

Joginder charged, full force, and nearly knocked the

whole wall down. They were out in less than 0.03 of a second. But they were not to meet beneath the trees at the back in 0.33 of a second. Or at any time after that. There were no trees. There was no grass, no grounds, no fields. They were in a big hall. The school hall. It looked like the Morning Assembly was in progress.

The entire school was gathered: teachers, pupils and office staff, as if for the Christmas service. The headmaster was at the podium, along with the deputy and a few senior teachers, while the rest of the hall was filled to capacity, with some pupils standing around by the sides or at the back. The school band and the choir were all in place.

The difference from Christmas was that, instead of everyone being in their glad rags, all were dressed in sombre black – black suits, black dresses, black cravats, black ties, black scarves, black veils and black hats. Black ribbons and black buntings were hanging from the doors and from the stage.

The black, however, was offset by the most colourful flowers littering the place. Bouquets of flowers, and baskets of flowers, and wreaths of flowers. Flowers all round. Hundreds and hundreds of flowers.

Ali took in the entire scene as soon as they entered the hall, for they were at the main door of it, at the back end, opposite the stage and facing it.

'We're here,' Ali shouted, and waved cheerily, expecting a big cheer to go round the hall from floor to ceiling and wall to wall. 'And we are alive!'

No response.

'I said we are alive,' Ali said again. 'And I am thirteen. Thirteen today. It is my birthday. Not my death day. No need to go through all this . . . all this, this, this . . . now is there?' Then he added, 'Thanks all the same,' considering all the trouble they had taken to commemorate their so-called death.

No one responded, yet again.

It was like being back in VSL. Nobody paid any attention to what he said.

Perhaps they were too far back for the Head and the senior staff to hear – the rest, with their backs to them, made no attempt to turn around and look. Ali started to walk up the aisle, to get closer, Joginder the elephant tagging behind.

The moment they took the first step, everyone began standing up – the pupils, the staff, the headmaster . . . in rows, like waves of a human sea. Human, but not for long. For as they stood, they changed. Some kept their faces, but their bodies turned into animal shapes. Others remained as they were from the neck down, but their faces started to sprout hair or fur or snouts; their eyes bulged till they were as large as snooker balls, or seemed to altogether disappear; or their heads grew horns – two, three, even more. Neither the metamorphosed bodies, nor the faces, belonged to any particular creature, but were a grotesque amalgam. And the process did not stop: the alterations continued, from limb to limb and feature to feature.

At the same time as all this was taking place, the band began to play a tune, strangely familiar, yet not quite right. It was only when the choir started to sing along that Ali got it.

It was Wagner's ever-popular 'Here comes the bride'. Only it was being played way too slow. And pretty much out of tune.

The words that accompanied the tune sounded weird, and they took a second or two to sink in.

> *The corpses are here*
> *The corpses are here . . .*

'Let's get the h—' Ali nearly said the H word, but his mother's face appeared in front of his eyes, larger than life, and he stopped himself. 'Let's get out of here. They are all mad!'

It was all too sick to be true. Ali's nightmares were coming to life.

As Ali tried to turn around, Joginder stopped him in his tracks, wrapping his trunk round his waist. The music and singing, if you could call it that, stopped along with them.

Joginder wasn't budging. As Ali turned to look at him, there were tears in his eyes, and before long his shoulders began to convulse, so violently that the whole hall began to shake to its very foundations.

Ali was moved to tears himself at Joginder's despair. 'There, there,' he said. 'Don't worry, I'll get you out of here. I'll find a way, you just wait . . .'

'Who *wants* to get out of here,' Joginder managed to blurt through his blubbing. 'This is the grandest reception I've ever had, grander than when I was decorated as a war hero. I cannot *leave* now! Cannot disappoint all these good creatures who—'

'You are crazy!' Ali shouted. 'All these *good creatures* are here to bury you. And me. I hate all schools and was half afraid I'd die in *this* rotten one. I never knew I'd live to see them burying me here. Well, I am not going to let them. I am not too, I will not let them bury me, even if I were dead. And neither will I let them bury you.'

So saying, Ali turned round and, holding Joginder by his ear, made a run for it. Or tried to. But failed. For Joginder wouldn't move an inch, and he was much too heavy for Ali to drag along, being a full-grown elephant, albeit an Indian, and not quite as large and cumbersome as an African might have been.

At that point, Ali decided that if Joginder refused to turn around, the best strategy would be to play along. Pretend to be dead. Walk gravely up the aisle to the dirge of 'The corpses are here', get in front of the stage, then leap up on it and down the actor's trapdoor hole – which was just by the side of the Head's chair. He didn't know how he knew that, but he knew that he knew, and that was enough for him to know. He could easily find his way out of there. He'd signal Joginder to follow him. If he did, well and good. If not, it was his funeral.

However, when they got to the stage, amid the monotonous bridal requiem that had restarted once they began their walk up the aisle, there was a problem. Between them and the proscenium stood an obstacle. Two obstacles, actually. Two coffins. One, about Ali's size; the other big enough for Joginder. And very attractive they were too. Ali was tempted. All that shouting and floating and falling and shouting and fear had quite exhausted him. And he was still drowsy from all those chemicals. It would be most relaxing to gently lie down in that plush coffin and go to sleep. In the lap of luxury. Lined with satin and velvet it was, white and purple and blue and gold, made of solid mahogany, with ivory inlay. The ivory, though, thought Ali, was in bad taste, considering Joginder. And unnecessarily extravagant, especially if they were to be cremated.

Ali shut his eyes tight to think, as he often did when he tried to think. There had to be a way out. There always is. No matter how bad the situation. His father always said. The thought of his father brought tears to his eyes, but he checked himself. He had to be strong. He could not give way to any weakness, not now, not in the situation he was in. Even his father, though not very sensible, would agree with that.

Just then, suddenly, with his shut eyes, he saw something he had not seen with his eyes open.

On the floor, to his right, in front of Joginder's coffin, was a red circle about the size of a man's head. Inside the circle was a big black X. Around the circle, in bold yellow letters, was written: PLEASE DO *NOT* STEP ON THIS!

Without waiting to think, Ali took a jump and landed directly on the cross, surprisingly able to drag Joginder along with him.

There was a sudden explosion and a thunderous boom. In less than a second everything disappeared: the stage, the Head and the staff, the pupils, the hall – everything!

Joginder and Ali were in the middle of a jungle. So thick, there was hardly room to stand; so dark, they could barely see each other.

But at last they were free. They could relax. Do what they wanted.

What Ali really wanted was to get home. Anything for a cold salad. He'd promise never to eat chips again. Never to think chips again. As for burgers . . . *never, never, never . . . only please, please, let me get home.*

But there seemed no way out of that jungle. He didn't know where to even begin looking. Joginder, who should have been at home in a jungle, looked equally bewildered.

Anyway, at least we're safe.

Not for long.

This is a public announcement, came the headmaster's voice, stridently making its way through the trees. *Two dead bodies have escaped from the Clunton-Flair School. One disguised as an Indian elephant, the other as an ugly schoolboy. They are armed, and legged, and very dangerous. This morning they exploded a bomb during their funeral ceremony, destroying the school hall and killing all the staff and pupils of the school. Fortunately they were all revived due to prompt action by the drum majorettes. The school hall has since been reconstructed, but still needs some good paintings for the north and east walls. Preferably of cows.*

The deceased escapees present a major health risk to our wildlife and the environment, indeed to our entire world. It is the civic duty of all members of the public to keep a look out for them, and give any information they might have about their whereabouts immediately and without any second thoughts, or indeed without any thought at all. Twenty million tons of garbage will be offered as a reward for their capture by the State Department of the Environment. Please remember, both bodies are seriously dead, and actively, treacherously, monstrously hazardous. If sighted, they must not be allowed to approach on any account. Simply contact your furthest police station. Twenty million tons of garbage can be yours. Tax free.

*

'Thank God we are here,' said Joginder.

'You would say that, wouldn't you,' said Ali sarcastically. 'Must be like home to you, this. Gives me the creeps.'

'Nothing *like* my home,' said Joginder, sounding hurt. 'I live in a two-bed seventy-seventh-floor flat in Beckenham. I mean, if they are out looking for us, it is safer in the forest here than anywhere else, wouldn't you say?'

'I wouldn't,' said a voice from nowhere, so suddenly and so unexpectedly it made Joginder jump a metre high in the air. Ali hid behind a tree in fear. 'Most trees here are plants,' continued the voice.

'Aren't all trees?' Joginder whispered timidly, not knowing where to look, for he couldn't see who the speaker was, or where.

'I mean *they* have planted them. As plants. I mean as *spies*. So you better watch where you go, or what you say, especially to a tree.'

'Who are you?' said Ali from behind the tree.

'Where are you?' said Joginder from under the tree.

'A friend,' said the voice from above the tree, 'and I am right here.'

It was the voice of an old black crow. The oldest, blackest crow in the forest. The oldest, blackest crow in the entire world. According to himself.

Joginder jerked his head up so hard it would have fallen off, had his neck not been so strong and so thick. Ali jerked his head up so hard it did fall off, his neck not being so strong and so thick – but he quickly picked it up and put it back on again, before the ants could get at it.

The whole of the jungle floor was beginning to crawl with ants. Big ants and small ants, and ants neither big nor small. Red ants and brown ants and black ants, and ants neither red nor brown nor black. And, of course, white ants.

'You better run for it,' said the crow, 'or these ants will eat you up. They love dead bodies, these ants, can smell them from—'

'BUT WE ARE *NOT* DEAD!' shouted Ali and Joginder at the same time, at the top of their voices.

'Maybe you are . . . maybe you are not . . .' said the old crow, looking straight down at them both and then looking away. 'I keep an open mind. If you are dead, the ants are here because of the smell, the smell of death. If you aren't dead but *they* say you're dead, then these must be the soldiers – I mean soldier ants – sent to capture you and take you to your funeral. Simple. Understand!' Here the old crow spoke very slowly, stressing every word, as if to a very small child or to a very stupid grown-up.

'I don't know where you are from,' said Ali, quite exasperated, 'but from where I am, dead people . . . or dead elephants, don't go about—'

'Talk later, run now,' screamed Joginder, and he started to run in a very funny manner, even for an elephant, shaking each leg like a salt shaker as he ran.

The ants were marching up his legs and beginning to bite, for although he had a smart grey jacket on, and even a perky little hat between the ears, he was trouserless. *Too much trouble, trousers*, he later confided in Ali, w*hat with my fat legs, and four of them at that!*

For once Ali was grateful to his school uniform. On a sunny day, like it was that morning, he might otherwise have been in shorts, perhaps even barefooted. He too began to run. In a matter of seconds he had outrun Joginder.

Should he stop and wait, like a true friend? Or should he carry on and save his skin?

Fortunately, the crow spared him from making a decision he might have regretted later. Swooping down on the elephant and holding on to him with both his claws, he flew up and away, shouting to Ali to follow.

'This way,' he said. 'There is a river nearby. Nothing but the water will save you from these ants.'

Ali ran as fast as he could. And he could run fast. Years of running from big bullying boys and big bullying girls in his old school in VSL had given him good practice. Being gawky and skinny may not be much good in a fight, but it was great for a sprint. Still, it was difficult to keep up with the flying crow. It would have been impossible were it not for the fact that the weight of the elephant was slowing the bird down a bit.

The 'nearby' must have been a very long way away, for although they kept running – or rather, *he* kept running – for what seemed like hours, there was no sign of the river . . . Gasping for breath and utterly, utterly exhausted, Ali was about to give up, lie down and let the ants devour him or the headmaster cremate him or whatever, when he heard a thunderingly resounding splash.

It was Joginder being dropped in the river.

'Thank God for that,' Ali managed to say between huffs and puffs, as he too jumped into the river, which suddenly appeared in front of him. 'It took ages to get here. I thought you said it was close!'

'It is all your fault,' the crow said in a sulky voice. 'I mean, if you'd got tired enough earlier, we'd have got here earlier. The river was only as far as you could run. And boy, can you run far! How d'you think it was for me, having to carry that big brute all the way through—? God, I thought you'd never tire! I mean, I thought I'd die before you tired! I thought the whole world would come to its end before you tired!'

'So it's *my* fault. Again. As always. It always is!' grumbled Ali as he half-swam, half-drowned in the river.

But it was a very soothing river, a peaceful river. What's more, it was a happy river.

Soon his tiredness was gone. Feeling fit as a sovereign and in a madly happy mood, he began singing his favourite songs. Surprisingly, Joginder and the crow knew the words and the tunes to all of them.

Before long, all the birds and animals, and most of the trees and bushes and grasses, and every variety of mushroom – poisonous and otherwise; red, white or spotted – joined in with Ali and Joginder and the crow, and the whole atmosphere was filled with joy and music. The trees clapped their leaves and crackled their branches. The river splashed its water about in a most rhythmic manner. Wild boars drummed on tree trunks. Squirrels and snakes, koalas and camels, reindeers and rats, and so many others it would take years to name them, all managed to dig out guitars and flutes and cymbals and violins and sitars and any other kind of musical instrument you can think of. Nightingales and skylarks sang notes so melodious no singer in the world ever had such a wonderful backing group. Nor so exciting an orchestra.

'Aaah . . . aaah . . . aaah! This is far better than singing in my bathtub up in my flat, with my rubber giraffe and 402 tank,' said Joginder while continuing to sing at the same time as he spoke, 'even though I hate to admit that anything anywhere is better than in my two-bed flat in Beckenham.'

Ali too was deliriously, ecstatically, unboundedly happier splattering about here than swimming his well-planned strokes in his well-ordered swimming pool at VSL.

So absorbed were they all in their music and song, and so uproariously loud, that they did not hear the helicopters approaching.

It was only when the helicopters started to close in and bear down that the crow caught sight and sound of them from the corner of his eye and ear. In one desperate swoop he was just able to carry both Ali and Joginder to safety on the west bank, no more than a split second before the helicopters dropped their heat bombs into the river, drying it all up in less than an instant.

'Wow! That was a narrow escape!' said Ali, looking down at the river bed, now so dry and parched you would have thought it had never seen water – not in the last two hundred years, maybe even three hundred.

'Wasn't it just!' Joginder piped in a tinny, scared voice, so unlike his normal boom. 'A second too late, and we would have been just carbon and ashes floating in the air.'

'If that!' whispered Ali under his breath, in awe at the sight of the barren river littered with skeletons of fish and crocodiles and whale and dolphins, still on fire. Hippo too!

'Ahem,' said the crow. 'Doesn't anyone here know a little word? Like thank you? This is the *second* time that I have—'

'*Thank you* is two words, not one,' said Ali. 'My mother gets very angry when you get your words mixed up or wrong!'

'Shouldn't it then be that thank you *are* two words and not *is*—' began Joginder.

But Ali interrupted. '*Thank you* may be *two* words, but it is *one* phrase, and as such—'

At this point the crow let out a squawk so loud and so scary that all the buildings in all the cities of the world shook as if there were an international earthquake, scale ninety-nine on the Richter scale. '*Will you two stop squabbling over words and phrases and tell me where you want to go now.* I have an important meeting in an hour, with the Health Minister, but I could drop you both off someplace before I fly away.'

'I want to go home, to my mother,' said Ali. 'I want to go to my flat in Beckenham,' said Joginder. Both at the same time.

'Since you two can't agree where you want to go, I will drop you off where I think fit!' said the crow and, swooping down, he picked up Ali, sat him on Joginder's back, and flew off with both of them.

Ali found himself falling fast and furiously, until he landed on a hard, smooth surface. He was in the blue-tiled corridor of the school. He knew it from the time he had been there with his mother. Fear grasped him by the throat. He was back in the *NoN* school. To be buried. Buried alive! Or roasted.

Just as he was about to turn back and run, a pair of large hands grasped him by the shoulders. He looked up to find himself staring into the eyes of a large, Indian gentleman. Ali almost screamed, but didn't. There was something familiar about the man, familiar and friendly. Before he could think of anything to say, the man smiled and said,

'Congratulations. You have passed your entrance test. Passed it brilliantly. You will be in the top set of your age group. Come, come with me. I will take you to your form room.'

Ali walked along with the man, almost in a trance, not knowing what to believe, and what not.

'By the way, my name is Mr Danesh. I will be your maths teacher.'

Ali felt a shiver run through his body. Maths teacher! Was it this huge chap who was going to sit on his head? Somehow the idea didn't seem quite as frightening now as it first had when the boy next door in the upside-down house had told him. He rather liked this man.

'Hi, Joginder,' said a pretty young woman carrying a pile of books on her carefully messy blonde head, a mug of coffee balanced precariously on top of the pile of books. 'Is this Ali Zaman, the new boy you were telling me about?'

Joginder nodded to the woman, smiled, then, turning to Ali, said, 'Miss Pfeffer. She'll be your science teacher.'

Ali liked her too. Very . . . sexy!

It wasn't going to be a bad birthday, after all.

For no reason at all, he patted the shiny green knapsack on his back and thought of his crazy grandmother.

Ali started walking home after school, still bewildered, but happy. It had been quite a day. Yes, quite a day . . .

He knew his mother would be out looking for a job somewhere, anywhere, and he had told her not to bother picking him up. She had sacrificed so much for him. If it hadn't been for him she could have stayed on in VSL, in her home, and kept her job. For she really was truly sensible. It was he who was the suspect one. Though he looked quite sensible and acted quite sensibly, there was always something about him – even he wasn't quite sure what – that aroused the suspicion of authorities, and some neighbours.

As he walked home he felt his knapsack getting heavier. Not very, but noticeably nonetheless. He almost thought of stopping and checking, but decided to wait till he got home. Which he did. Sitting on his doorstep, he slipped the knapsack off his shoulders and unzipped its top.

Something jumped out of it so vigorously that Ali fell over backwards with the sheer force of it – not to mention the utter surprise.

As soon as he could get his breath and senses back, he saw what had so energetically escaped out of the knapsack.

It was a big blue bike. Just the type he had always dreamed of.

Their battered old car drove up outside their door. Linta stepped out with a bounce, rushed up to Ali, who was still sitting spellbound on his doorstep, and hugged him hard to herself. 'I've got a job. Your unlucky thirteenth has been very lucky. It's only a . . . small . . . job, nothing important, but it will pay the rent, and leave me enough time to be with you.'

Ali was so happy for his mother that he even forgot about his bike. 'What will you be doing, Mum?'

'Littering,' said Linta, somewhat sheepishly. 'I'll be given a council truck, full of garbage, all sorts of rubbish, whatever, and then I'll go round littering the streets, parks, places . . . A new route every week, so it won't get too tedious and samey. There'll be another truck behind picking it all up again. My main job will be to make it as difficult as possible for them to find everything I dump. Two hours every morning, and one in the evening.'

She somehow looked different. There was a new note in her voice. A certain glint in her eyes Ali hadn't seen for ages.

'I will have an hour's head start, an assistant and quite a few gadgets to help disperse the rubbish as erratically as possible or secrete it in hard-to-locate places so as to make it tricky for the second truck to get to it. Any that is left behind will be added to my salary as bonus.'

'That's the best birthday present I could ever have had. The best birthday I could ever have had,' said Ali, jumping up and down then standing on his head and laughing hysterically with his feet wide apart in the air.

'But you haven't even seen what I have brought for you!' said Linta, sounding more like her usual self.

Ali didn't care. He was sure it would be most wonderful, no matter what it was.